Our Long Road Home

A Story of a Migrant Farm Family
During the Great Depression

A biographical novel

Don Morgan Edwards

ISBN 978-1-956001-92-1 (paperback)
ISBN 978-1-956001-93-8 (eBook)

Printed in the United States of America

A Human Interest Novel of a Rural Farm Family
Set in the 1920's and 30's

Prologue

At the beginning of the 1920's, America was going through a dramatic social and political change. As well, the high-spirited and free-wheeling urban population was undergoing a great cultural change. Henry Ford had recently begun the mass production of the automobile, requiring a large work force. The younger urban population ushered in a new type of dance; women could now vote; the styles of dress for men and women had drastically changed; and they had rejected many of the traditional moral standards.

This was the 'Jazz' age and an economic boom for much of the country. However, this economic boom did not extend into the farming community which still made up almost half of the Nation's population. The farmers had been accustomed to feeding the U.S. Army and most of Europe. But, now that WWI was over and the European farmers were back to work on their farms there was no longer a demand for the large quantity of U. S. farm produce. Therefore, prices collapsed and with the governmental imposed tariffs it was very difficult for the American farmers to sell produce overseas. With the ending of the war, the Great Depression began for the farmer. Many of them lost their farms and some began migrating to the cities in an attempt to fine employment.

Chapter One

Zolie's Pa, John Morgan Edwards, sometimes called Jessie, was not home and had been gone for four days. The family were all worried that something bad had happened to him. Zolie was the oldest son still living at home, so he took it upon himself to go and try to locate his Pa.

Zolie walked for a couple of miles, stopping at each farm, asking if anyone had seen his pa. He then came to a small, shabby house. He stepped onto the rickety porch and knocked on the door. He was shocked when his Pa answered. From where Zolie stood, he could see into the meager kitchen area were a stunningly beautiful, brown-skinned pregnant woman was standing with a small child holding around one of her legs.

Disbelief flooded over Zolie as he took in everything that he was seeing and then he blurted out, "what are you doing here, Pa? You ain't been home for four days and Ma has been worried sick!"

Pa yelled. "You watch your mouth, young'un, I'm your Pa and I ain't standing here and letting you speak to me that way. Git over here and let me teach you some manners, I'll show you."

His Pa was heading toward a razor strap hanging on the wall, and Zolie knew what that meant. He was going to whip him, so Zolie quickly jumped off the porch and ran back home.

When Zolie got home he was embarrassed and disgusted, but he knew that he had to tell his Ma. "I found Pa shacked up with a young, very pregnant woman and she already has another young'un. The girl looked not much older than I do. Pa and I argued a little and Pa started to get the strap so I ran. I'm never going to let Pa whup me again so I'm going to run away from home where he will never find me."

His ma had several young ones that could help her with the farm chores so Zolie thought he could find work and send his ma money when he could. His older sister and brothers had already left home.

John, Zolie's Pa, was a handsome, strong Scotsman with a straight stature, broad shoulders, and large hands and he had piercing blue eyes and coal-black hair. He must have been very charming with the ladies-of-the-night. But, finding him cheating on his mom taught Zolie to never be unfaithful to his wife, if he ever got married!

As a strong willed, stubborn and very angry 15-year-old man, Zolie Morgan Edwards started his life of loneliness and surviving on his own. He was not afraid of hard work and was determined to help his mom financially with raising his younger siblings. He soon got a job toiling as a hired laborer on the farms in north western Tennessee.

After several years of being on his own and only talking to the cows, and occasionally to his boss, he was getting desperate to meet someone nearer his own age. But, working from sunrise to dark had left little time to socialize.

That was the moment he knew it was time for him to settle down. He just needed to find someone to settle down with. He had saved up some money during the years that he had worked and he also had learned a lot about farming. Zolie didn't want to live in Tennessee where his pa and all of his relatives lived so he saddled his horse and headed west. He found a little farm that he could rent as a share-cropper in north eastern Arkansas so that's where he settled down. Zolie found out that there were other families living close by and that they were originally from Tennessee, near the place where he was born.

But loneliness still followed him. He recalled the Bible saying that man should not live alone.

Zolie was told that the farm he had rented had already been planted in cotton and that the owner had previously had an accident and was unable to harvest. After Zolie finished picking cotton and settling up with the owner, he decided to go to a near-by farm where he heard that a party was scheduled. It was the custom in this part of Arkansas that on Saturday nights after all the chores were done, the young people would have a get-to-gather at one of the farms.

He was now 22 years of age but rather shy around girls. When he got to the party he looked around and immediately saw a pretty young Irish girl standing alone near the back of the room. Zolie was reluctant to walk up to her, being the shy type. She appeared to be much younger than Zolie and he figured that being out on his own for several years and having had years of life experiences he was worried that he might frighten her because of his age. And also, because he was the new guy in town.

When the party was winding down, the young girl walked up to Zolie and said, "I have seen you around town for a while. You must be the guy that is now farming the old Mosley farm east of town."

"I didn't know that you would even notice me," Zolie replied.

"I saw you when you came in a while ago," she replied. "I had a fuss with my boyfriend and he left me stranded. Would you like to walk me home?"

They started seeing each other every chance that they had and soon fell in love. After 3 months, they were married at the town's court house. Zolie's lovely young wife was 17 years old. Zolie's name was Zolie Morgan Edwards and his wife's name was James Rosa McCain, now Edwards. His nick-name for her soon became "Jim" and she always called him, "Bud". Hence, the two of them began their lives together.

Chapter Two

For their first breakfast as a married couple, Zolie's wife Jim cooked biscuits and gravy.

"I couldn't find any eggs or pork to cook, so I made some biscuits and gravy," Jim stated, with a smile. "Will that do?"

"Jim, I've been wondering, how come your first name is James?" Zolie asked, trying not to hurt her feelings or embarrass her.

"Well, my mom died when I was only five years old," Jim began. "She was a young woman but already had six kids, all girls. My dad badly wanted a boy so before I was born Dad named me 'James'. After I was born a girl, he added the name Rosa."

"Rosa is a pretty name but I think that I will continue to call you Jim, if that is alright with you," Zolie replied.

"That's fine and I will continue to call you Bud," She replied with a sweet grin.

"What about your family?" Jim asked. "You are not from around here. Where are you from?"

"I was born in Northwestern Tennessee near McKenzie and grew up there," Bud answered. "I left home when I was fifteen and worked on farms there until I moved out here."

"What a small world, I was born near Sharon in Weakley County," Jim said. My mom had another baby girl, Annie, after I was born. After Annie was born, my Mom was bed-fast and after being bed-fast for a year she died."

"Your dad had to raise all you girls by himself!" Bud sympathetically said.

"No, my dad found an 18 year-old girl to marry and to help raise us girls," Jim angrily replied. "When my dad was away at work my step-mother would make me and my three sisters go outside and then she would lock the doors until just before it was time for Dad to come home. She wouldn't feed us anything after breakfast so we girls would hide pieces of cornbread in our dress pockets so we wouldn't get hungry during the long afternoons. One of my older married sisters found out about the terrible way our step-Mother was treating us and brought me and Annie here to Arkansas to live with her. Later my dad moved out here also."

"I'm sorry you had such a tough time growing up," Bud said. "I also had some troubles before I left home. I come from a large family. I have three older brothers and an older sister and three younger sisters and four younger brothers. I just suddenly left home one day. I'll tell you about it sometime."

Chapter Three

"I've been talking to some of the neighbors and everyone thinks that the price of cotton should hold because of the war," Bud said to Jim, while they ate dinner under the shade of a tree next to the cotton field. "With our first young'un on its way, you should stop bringing my dinner to the field every day at noon, you should slow down some."

"Don't be silly," Jim said. "Having a baby is just as natural as getting up in the morning. I'll be alright. My aunt lives less than three miles away, and she told me it was o.k."

That fall the cotton crop was good but the price per pound had fallen to 6.8 cents, almost half of what it was the year before, which was a real blow especially with their first baby due in February.

"Bud, I want my aunt to be with me when the baby comes," Jim said in early February. "She raised me and she is like my mom."

Zolie saddled his horse and rode over to the McCain farm. As soon as he delivered Rosa's message he left their farm and hurried back home. Rosa's aunt asked Zolie questions about how far along Rosa was but he didn't know the answers since this was all new to him. Mr. McCain hitched up the buggy and he and his daughter got to the Edwards' farm shortly after Zolie had arrived.

It was a little after five on a cold Friday morning February 15, 1915, when Zolie heard a baby cry. They had sent word to the doctor in Marmaduke that Rosa was about ready to deliver and the doctor arrived just in time. Zolie was now the proud papa of a baby boy, who they named Olie Morgan, after Zolie.

Eastern Arkansas was wet, cold and swampy. Olie had a difficult time breathing and didn't seem to be growing as Zolie and Rosa expected. They asked the neighbors if they knew of any remedy for his slow growth and breathing problems. Zolie and Rosa began trying every herb and remedy that anyone suggested. The new parents waited for spring to come and hoped that warm, summer weather would be more agreeable for Olie.

*****

Now that WWI was nearing an end, it was getting more and more difficult to make it on the small share-crop farm and the Edwards family was struggling. The crop looked good but the price of cotton was still low. Rose was pregnant with their second baby. It was a hot and dry Sunday on August 5, 1917, when Zolie heard a new-born baby cry for the second time. He was now the proud papa of a baby girl.

The year after OlaB, their baby girl, was born there was an outbreak of the flu. Everyone was getting very sick. Zolie went from neighbor to neighbor tending to the sick. There was hardly a household that didn't have someone stricken with the flu. The neighbors, who weren't sick, would cut wood and pile it on the sick folk's porches so they would have wood to cook and keep warm.

There was a funeral almost every day in and around Paragould, Arkansas. Rosa would cook pots of beans and pans of cornbread and Zolie would leave the food on the neighbor's front porch. Some of the neighbors would milk the sick neighbors' cows and feed their stock and gather their eggs and whatever else there was to do except go into their homes.

"Bud, would you go over and check on my dad and sister," Jim asked.

"Sure, I'll be happy to drop by their place and take them a pot of beans and some cornbread," Bud answered. "Jim, you realize that at your dad's age this flu probably will turn into pneumonia. I'll stop in and see what they need."

From that point on, Zolie went into his sick neighbor's houses and helped feed them and do whatever he could to make them more comfortable. He sat up long hours, day and night, giving the sick the medicines the doctor had left. He kept his mouth and nose covered with a handkerchief and frequently washed his hands but finally he also was stricken with the flu.

Zolie stayed in the back room of their house and Rose would set his food on a table by the bed. Rose now had all the work to do around the farm by herself. By now every home had someone sick so there was no one left to help others. Rose was not strong but she was a real trooper and had to keep everything going. Thankfully, some of the neighbor men or boys helped her by keeping firewood on the porch.

Zolie began to get better and after a couple of weeks he was able to get up and do around. He went into town and learned the shocking news that nation-wide almost 700,000 people had died from the flu.

*****

Zolie was steadily recovering, regaining his strength when Olie came down with pneumonia. After about two weeks his fever left but he was very weak. He got up and played but his fever returned and didn't go away in spite of everything the doctor tried. This lasted for nine months and the doctor told them that the only thing left was to operate on Olie's lungs.

"He is too weak to stand an operation," Bud said, as he and Jim discussed the doctor's recommendation. "We will wait a while."

Zolie went in search of another doctor that he had heard about in a nearby town. The word was that this doctor was having good success treating lung disorders using a different method. He agreed to come and examine Olie. He was German and the U.S. had just ended the war with Germany. With a prayerful heart, Zolie and Rosa let the stranger examine Olie, and he insisted on being alone while he was examining Olie.

Doctor John came into the room where the young parents were sitting and told them that their small son would not need an operation and that he could make Olie well. He told them that he would need to see Olie every day for a while. Being a German, Doctor John did not have many patients, because people were still leery of him. He and his wife could not have children so he sort of adopted Olie.

Doctor John traveled everywhere with his side-kick, a collie dog. On one of his visits, he let the dog come in to visit Olie. It was love at first sight!

"If you take the tonic, without fussing, I will give you one of her puppies for your very own," Dr. John said.

"But the tonic tastes awful," Olie squealed.

"Remember, you have to take it without fussing," the doctor said. "This did the trick to get Olie taking his medicine."

Olie was soon able to get out of bed. But, he had to learn to walk all over again. The doctor told them that Olie would eventually outgrow the disorder and live normally.

Several weeks later, Doctor John brought a puppy on one of his visits. Olie was overjoyed, he now had a dog of his very own.

"What are you going to name your little puppy?" Doctor John asked.

"I am going to name him 'John' after you," Olie answered.

His new playmate, the collie, John, became a member of the Edwards' household on that day. He became the constant playmate and protector of Olie and OlaB. Rosa could tell by John's bark whether a person or another animal got close to her babies by the difference in his barking.

Doctor John's practice grew by leaps and bounds as word got out about Olie's recovery. Doctor John had to farm to make a living, because no one had money to pay him. He was paid with things to eat or things to use. His doctoring took all of his time so he soon had to give up on farming altogether.

"Mr. Edwards," Dr. John asked soon after he realized that he had to give up farming. "I have been thinking that I don't have time to farm anymore and was wondering if you would consider working for me and farming my land?"

I will need to talk this over with my wife and get back to you," Zolie replied.

Rosa and Zolie both thought that this was a good idea so they began working for Dr. John.

Chapter Four

The Move to Mississippi—

"Jim, we could stay here and work for Doctor John," Bud said one evening in early spring after returning home from Doctor John's farm. "I was thinking maybe we should move to a better climate. Olie was awful sick last winter and a dryer place might be good for him. We can't make a living farming these days. If we have another winter like last winter none of us might make it. Jim, what do you think?"

"You are going to have to make that decision, Bud," Jim answered. "I will go wherever you decide is best."

"I was thinking that maybe we should move out of this damp swampy country and go to some place dryer," Bud continued. "It would mean leaving your family."

"I'll be willing to go away from here if it means helping Olie," Jim said. "We have to do what's best for our family."

"I have a brother in Mississippi," Bud replied. "I could write him and have him rent us a big place where we could try our luck at raising horses."

Zolie and Rosa excitedly talked it over and decided that the move to Mississippi would be good for all of them. The next day Zolie went into town and bought a little lumber, some nails, a rope and a few other things. He also put all of their livestock up for sale, keeping two of his best horses, some chickens and Olie's pet collie, 'John'. While in the process of selling the livestock, Zolie met an older man by the name of John Thomas. They struck up a conversation and found that they both had a lot in common.

"I've never been married and have saved some money," John said, as the two men continued to get acquainted with each other. "I have been teaching school for the past several years and want to try my hand at farming and raising horses."

"I'm here to sell my livestock and move to Mississippi," Zolie said. "I have been thinking about raising and training horses myself. You just can't make a living farming these days."

John Thomas and Zolie decided to form a partnership. John was willing to finance the partnership and Zolie would run the operation.

*****

Zolie built boxes and fastened them around the outside of their wagon to carry the cooking utensils and supplies. One box was for dishes, one was for skillets and pots, and one was for their food and another for clothes and bedding. He and Rosa didn't have many household goods but Zolie sold everything that they could do without.

John Thomas followed alongside the wagon with his horse and a few things he had packed on a pack mule.

"How long should it take us to get to your brothers place?" Rosa asked, and John repeated the question anxiously.

"Well, travel is going to be very slow," Zolie replied. "On a dry sunny day we might be able to make as much as twenty miles. It's summer now, so we shouldn't be bothered with any big storms."

"I'll write my sister a good-bye letter to let her know that we are now leaving for Mississippi," Rosa said, with a little tremor to her voice.

"Jim, I'm sorry we'll be taking you away from your sister and her family," Bud said sympathetically. "I know you think of her as your Ma, since she raised you from the time your Ma died and you were just a young'un."

The Edwards family were now on their way to Mississippi. OlaB rode up front in the wagon, mostly snuggled on Rosa's lap. Rosa made a pallet for Olie on the wagon bed right behind the wagon seat. It was hard to keep him still, he was always getting up so he could see what was going on. He was very curious and full of questions!

By mid-afternoon on the fifth day, they ferried across the Mississippi River, much to Olie's wonder, and by nightfall they were setting up camp in the state of Mississippi. The weather was wet and sticky, just like back in Arkansas. Zolie was hoping that the further they got from the river the damp weather would get better. Things began to look up, on the third day after leaving the river the wind started to blow and cool things off a bit. They were beginning to get into some rolling hills covered in trees. The hills smoothed out as they neared Zolie's brother's place. This is going to be our new home, Zolie thought.

Chapter Five

Zolie had written his brother in Mississippi and told him about what time to expect them. He mentioned that his partner, John Thomas, would be moving with them. Zolie also asked his brother if he could find time to start plowing the fields because they may not get there in time to get the fields ready to plant. In exchange for getting the fields ready to plant, Zolie told his brother that he would give him part of the year's crop. His brother agreed and wrote Zolie that as soon as he finished his planting, he would move over to Zolie's farm and start plowing.

Once Zolie and his family arrived and got settled and the horses had rested for a couple of days, he started working the Mississippi farm. It didn't take long for Zolie to learn that John Thomas had never farmed and had no idea of what to do. Zolie spent several days having John follow him and learn what needed to be done. Zolie wasn't sure that John would ever be much of a farmer.

The house was big enough for all of the Edwards and John to live in, so John became another member of the Edwards' household. He loved kids, and having been a teacher, he was able to teach Olie how to count and recite his ABC's. When Olie and OlaB got a little older he began to teach them how to read.

Zolie tried teaching John how to hitch the horses to a plow, but soon learned that John was terribly afraid of horses. Especially when a 'near accident' happened when he got too close to the back-end of one of the horses.

The crop that year was good but prices of cotton was still too low and Zolie was afraid that the family couldn't make a living. The place in Mississippi was just not large enough to raise horses, as planned; so, besides farming, Zolie decided to raise a few goats. He still wasn't really sure that they could make a living just by adding a few goats to the farm. It soon became evident that it was costing more to keep the goats than they made from selling their milk for cheese. Rosa and Zolie discussed the situation and Zolie decided that he had to think about finding something else to do. But, farming was the only thing that he knew. The way it looked, with the price of cotton so low, they would just have enough money to make another crop for the next year.

*****

For Olie's fifth birthday Zolie and Rose got him a little red wagon. He loved the wagon and chased his dog 'John' around in the barnyard while pulling it.

"So, would you like to have a little goat for your own?" Zolie asked Olie.

"I would, I would," Olie replied jumping up and down with a smile as big as a full-moon on his face. "And, Papa, I will name him Billy."

"I'll make a harness to fit 'Billy'," Zolie said the next morning. "That way Billy will be able to pull you around too."

That spring Olie and Billy were inseparable. When not hitched up to the red wagon, Billy would follow Olie and Olie's pet dog, John, everywhere they went, but sometimes, it was the other way around.

One Sunday afternoon, Zolie, Rose, Olie and OlaB were all in the wagon going over to Zolie's brother's farm for Sunday dinner, when one of the back wheels of the wagon hit a rock. Olie and Billy were on the back of the wagon and Billy was bounced out. Olie began hollering over and over to STOP. Zolie got the wagon stopped and ran to the back to see what all of the raucous was about.

"Papa," Olie cried. "Billy fell out of the wagon and can't get up."

"It's OK, son," he said. "It doesn't look like Billie's hurt bad. See he's trying to get up but can't seem to put any weight on his front leg. I'll go pick up him up and we'll see how hurt he is."

"Here, help me son," Zolie said as he looked for two small branches to use as splints.

Ollie and Zolie found what they needed on a nearby tree and Zolie tied the small limbs onto Billy's left front leg.

"See there, Billy's as good as new," Zolie reassured Olie. "In a few weeks Billy will be pulling you around in your little red wagon again."

*****

Zolie was usually finished by supper time and back at the house in time to feed and milk the cows and goats. But one day, since it was going to be almost dark before he could finish, he had asked Rosa to do the milking that evening.

"I am going out to do the milking this evening," Rosa told Olie and OlaB. "Olie, I want you to look after your little sister while I am out at the barn."

Rosa took both kids with her to gather the eggs and feed the chickens but when it was time to milk she took them to the house, knowing that OlaB was afraid of the cows. She sat Olie in a chair on one side of the room and OlaB in a chair on the other side. She told them not to move out of their chairs and that she would be back shortly.

When Rosa returned to the house with the milk buckets, she found Olie and OlaB just where she had left them except OlaB didn't have any hair. Rosa was too busy when she first got back to the house and strained the milk and getting it put in a cool place. She hadn't looked at Olie or OlaB until she called them in for their night meal.

Rosa discovered that while she was milking, Olie had climbed down from his chair and drug it over to where a pair of scissors was kept hanging on the wall on a nail. When he had finished with OlaB's haircut he cut a big handful of hair off his own head.

When Rosa saw Olie and OlaB she didn't say a word. She just went out to the peach tree and got a switch and wore it out on both kids. When Zolie got home and finished his supper he looked at Olie and OlaB and went out to the same peach tree and got another switch. And such was life in Mississippi.....

*****

The next year the crop was good but prices were still too low for Zolie and Rosa to make a living. John and Zolie discussed the fact that it was absolutely impossible make to make a living by farming.

"I still have some money left to invest since we haven't bought any horses yet," John said, trying to find some solution. "I still want to raise horses even though I am still afraid of them."

"I think that there is a great demand for horses and I think that we could make a pretty good living raising and training them," Zolie replied. "I am pretty good when it comes to breaking horses. We would have to find a much larger place if we intend to raise horses though."

"I have been making some inquiries and I think that I have found a place in Missouri," John continued. "The place is mostly level grass land and I believe that it would be excellent for what we want to do."

"John, can you write your contact in Missouri and get the particulars of this farm?" Zolie asked. "I will talk it over with Jim."

John and Zolie continued to talk about the move. That evening Zolie approached Rosa as they were getting ready for bed.

"This farm ain't working out, we are just getting farther in a hole," said Zolie. "We have to do something different. John has heard of a place in Missouri where we can raise and train horses. I think that it is something that we should try. Jim, what do you think?"

"Well," Rosa answered. "We have not accumulated much stuff in the two years that we have been here, so moving again wouldn't be much different than when we left Arkansas. What will your brother say?"

"I don't think that it will bother him any," Zolie answered. "He's having trouble making ends meet, same as us."

The Edwards family and John Thomas loaded up the wagon and they all headed for Missouri hoping for a better life.

Chapter Six

Move to Missouri—

It was mid-October when Zolie and his family left his brother's place in Mississippi. They had not accomplished much in the way of making a living during the two years that they lived there. Now, they were headed for a farm that John Thomas, Zolie's business partner, had heard about near the Missouri-Kansas state line. It was located about 15 miles from Pittsburg, Kansas. Zolie hoped to get there before bad weather set in. He would rather have started their move nearer to the first of October, but the sale of their goats had delayed their move. It took longer to gather all of the supplies which they would need and get the wagon loaded for the long trip. The trip would be hard on Rosa and the two young children and it would take about a month—if the weather stayed mild.

During the first week of their trip, the weather was good and they made about 20 miles each day. However, supplies were running low and after Zolie and John set up camp one evening, John rode into a town nearby to pick up the few supplies which they needed. When he returned, he hurriedly and excitedly reported that he had overheard some people talking about a storm that was headed their way.

By morning as they broke camp in a light drizzle, Zolie and John commented that they hoped that the shower would not turn into a down-pour and make the road impassable. The rain was cold so Zolie stopped and pulled a tarp up over the wagon seat and the four Edwards huddled close to one another for warmth. They made only about 10 miles before stopping and letting the horses rest for the night. The rain finally stopped after a few days. Indian summer was definitely over. Days turned into weeks and the weather continued to get colder. By the middle of November they finally arrived at their destination in Missouri.

John had been given general directions to the farm which they had rented, but he was not sure that he had found the right place. Zolie stayed with his family in the wagon while John rode up ahead on horse-back going farther down the dirt road, which was really nothing but a lane. About half a mile from the wagon, John came upon a nice farm. After he introduced himself to the owners, the Peters, he showed Mr. Peters the information that he had been given and asked if he could tell him how to find the location. Mr. Peters laughingly told John that he must have passed the farm that he was looking for but that no one was living there and hadn't lived there for a couple of years. John told Mr. Peters that he and Zolie Edwards, his partner, and Zolie's family had rented the farm and they would be his new neighbors.

John returned to the wagon and told Zolie that the large farm house that they had just passed was actually the house that they were looking for and that it had been vacant for some time.

It was almost dark, and getting colder by the minute, so Zolie and John unloaded only what they would need for the night. They decided to wait to unload the rest until morning. Olie, being a curious little boy, was so excited to be able to run and play that he had not noticed that it had begun to snow.

Zolie found some wood outside near the barn, suitable for building a fire, and soon they were warm and ready for Rosa's hurriedly prepared supper. First, she had to clean cob-webs and dust from the cook-top, but she was an accomplished housekeeper, especially when everyone was starved for a home-cooked meal.

Rats had been living in the house for some time and had chewed holes in the plaster walls. That night Rosa made pallets on the floor in front of the fireplace for a bed for Olie and OlaB to sleep. Neither of the children could go to sleep in another new house, and not being in their own beds. Olie was too excited and wanted to explore while OlaB was afraid that the rats would come and scratch and bite her in her sleep. Finally, their fidgeting was overcome by fatigue and the children settled down and both went to sleep.

OlaB woke up during the night screaming and crying. The rats were running in the open spaces in the walls making loud scratching noises and one of them ran out into the room waking her up. After killing the rat with a broom handle and setting a rat trap, Zolie beat out some tobacco cans and nailed them to cover the rat holes. He repeated this process for the next few nights until all the holes were covered and more traps were set.

The next morning they awoke to a thin blanket of snow covering the ground. Zolie and John unloaded the wagon and helped Rosa and the kids settle into the new house.

Zolie and Rosa had very little in the way of furniture. In the living room there was a rocking chair for each of the adults. In addition, there were tables with a coal-oil lamp setting on the tables by each rocking chair. The fireplace and the lamps shed the only light in the room. A lamp would be moved to the bedroom or kitchen when light was needed. A sewing machine was next to one of the lamp tables. Olie's and OlaB's bed rooms had a bed, a chair, and a trunk in which to keep their clothes. Mirrors were hanging on the wall above each of the trunks.

In the kitchen there was a long table which Zolie had previously made out of lumber that he had found lying around the Mississippi farm. The table was set in the middle of the kitchen and was always covered with a red checked oilcloth, except when meals were finished, then the table was covered with a clean white cloth.

The house had a large black wood-burning cook stove with a large tank on the side which was kept filled with water. Zolie made a small table that sat by the stove where Rosa would prepare meals. He made selves above the table to hold kitchen supplies. On a second set of shelves, the plates, cups and glasses were kept.

*****

"It looks like everything in here is all set and ready to live in," Zolie said to John as they finished the construction of the kitchen selves. "I think we should ride into Pittsburg early tomorrow morning. What do you think?"

"That's a great idea," John replied. "I am anxious to see what we can find."

They left for Pittsburg, Kansas, the next morning with the intent of buying horses and starting the horse business. On the way, they talked it over and decided that a lot needed to be done at the farm before bringing any horses home. They decided not to start the horse farm until spring so they went to the stock yard and bought a few head of cattle and some hogs, which were ready to be butchered.

Pittsburg, Kansas, was only 15 miles west of their farm and was known for its coal mining. The mine employed a lot of men. Several of the men had families living with them so Zolie and John started a butchering business that winter. They could butcher during the day and take the meat to the mines by the time the men got off work. Since the days were cold, the meat would last a day or so before spoiling.

Business was doing well, or so Zolie thought. However, many of the miners had told John that they didn't have money on them so John let them have the meat on credit. John was in charge of the finances and the book keeping. One day not too long after the start of the butchering business, Zolie noticed that the books were in the red. He asked John about the losses and learned about the credit John had been issuing. They lost a lot of money that winter until Zolie made a decision to butcher and sell only on consignment. It was not Zolie's intention to go into the business of raising hogs, but he kept a few. One problem solved!

Olie was interested in everything that was going on including butchering. He was especially fascinated watching the hogs each day. One of the sows had a liter of piglets and she took a dislike to one of them. She would hardly let it suckle with the others and it wasn't growing and was getting weaker by the day.

Zolie told Olie, "you can have this runt pig for your own if you take good care of it and feed it every day."

"Yeah, I'll take really good care of it, Pa, since I don't have my little goat, Billie, any longer, I will have plenty of time," Olie said excitedly.

The little pig grew to a large sow with Olie's tender, loving care. It was soon grown and become mean-tempered so Zolie took it to market. He brought back the money he received for it and handed it to Olie. Olie was thrilled to have some money all his own in his pocket, for the first time.

The winter was cold and large drifts of snow packed against the house. There was a lot more snow than Zolie or Rosa had ever seen before. Even though Olie wanted to go outside and play in the snow, Rosa was afraid to let him because of his lung condition.

One night in early January, OlaB woke up having a nightmare about the rats. She had a low fever and was having trouble breathing. She also complained of a pain in her chest. This frightened Zolie and Rosa because they remembered the flu epidemic that occurred a few years before and because Olie had had so much trouble with his lungs. OlaB had never experienced anything like this before. Zolie built a fire and left Rosa walking the floor with OlaB.

Zolie made his way to the barn in blizzard conditions and saddled his horse. He had heard that almost every winter someone would get lost in a blizzard and freeze to death. He slowly worked his way through the snow to the Peter's farm. The Peters were the only people in the area with a phone and the only ones who had a car. When Zolie finally got to their farm he called the only doctor in Pittsburg. When the doctor answered the phone Zolie explained OlaB's condition.

"I don't think that I could find your farm at night in this blizzard, the doctor said. "I'm afraid that I might get lost and freeze to death. I only have a horse and buggy as transportation."

"I don't think she can make it much longer if she can't breathe, what can we do to help her?" Zolie anxiously asked.

"Boil some water and have her breath the steam," the doctor answered. "Give her a teaspoon of whisky and put a heated cloth on her chest, continuing this through the night, and I will be by your place in the morning at first light."

During the night, OlaB's fever broke and her breathing became regular. Rose slept beside her in her bed but watched closely over her for the rest of the night.

Zolie called the doctor the next morning and told him that OlaB was better, he thanked him for his advice, and told him that now he wouldn't be needed.

Chapter Seven

Spring finally arrived and John and Zolie went shopping for horses. They were looking for good, hearty draft horses, ones that could be trained to pull a wagon or buggy as well as a plow. Zolie had a good eye for the type of horse flesh that they needed. They bought four horses and brought them home. John, being afraid of horses, left Zolie to do most of the training and all of the breaking.

That spring the two partners planted corn to help supplement the hay which they would make from the pasture. It soon became more and more evident that John was no farmer, although he was learning. He really didn't know what to do and Zolie had to show him almost everything.

"John, I can't keep doing all the breaking and training that I need to do and help you with the farming too," Zolie told him. "We need some help. Go to town tomorrow and try to locate some young man to help you with the farming. That way, I can devote all my time training the horses."

"I'll leave first thing after breakfast," John replied. "I'm sure that I will be able to find some young man that wants to make an extra dollar."

"Make dead sure that he has some experience farming or at least is willing to learn," Zolie said. "That's how I learned to do things as a young'un around a farm back in Tennessee."

That afternoon John returned home with a young man, about 18 years old, named Bert. Zolie and John showed Bert around the farm and told him what he would be expected to do. Bert was eager and willing to do almost anything and was very happy to have a job. The house was big enough for Bert to live in also, so, they offered him board and room as a part of his salary.

That spring and summer everyone worked and did their share. Olie and OlaB had their jobs to do also. OlaB's job was to keep the wood box behind the cook stove filled at all times. Olie would help her gather the wood from the wood pile in back of the house. They had to keep corn cobs in a can of coal oil to soak overnight so their Pop could start a fire every morning so Mom could cook breakfast. Another job of theirs was to keep the water bucket full and setting on the table by the back door.

Rosa raised hundreds of geese. During the molting season in July, Olie and OlaB helped collect the goose down from the roost. They would also hold the geese while Rosa would brush and comb the bird removing the down. Olie delighted in chasing the geese trying to catch one of them. He would laugh when one of the geese began chasing OlaB, biting at her heals. In the fall Rosa would ride along with Zolie on a full two-day's trip, taking several geese to Pittsburg to the slaughter house. The trip was done in time for the Christmas market in the larger eastern cities. Most of the country was in a prosperous, fun-loving and joyful frame of mind now that World-War-One was over.

However, the prosperity experienced by most of the country was not felt by farmers. Most small farmers grew most of what they ate. What little money they had was spent to replace a few pair of overalls or a pair of shoes for most family members each year. Very little money was left for repairing or replacing worn-out farm equipment.

Life on the farm started before sunrise. Zolie would get up thirty minutes before Rosa and get a fire started in the cook-stove and in the fireplace during the colder months. He and Olie would leave for the barn with milk buckets to milk the cows and feed the stock before Zolie had to take Olie to school after they ate their breakfast. OlaB would help

Rosa with breakfast, consisting of biscuits with gravy made from either the sausage, bacon or ham drippings. There was always eggs, jelly and butter. Rosa would skim off the top cream and put it in the churn with a long dasher. OlaB would plunge the dasher up and down until butter would form. After adding a little salt and after working all of the milk out of the mix, Rosa would mold the butter into one pound bricks, saving back what they would eat, and selling the rest to the miners. This was an everyday routine.

In back of the barn was a shack built over a small spring of water and partially buried in the side of a hill. The water ran year-round and the 'spring house' would house and keep the garden vegetables fresh along with the eggs, butter and milk. Also, the cured and smoked meat was kept in this house for several months.

In the fall, when the weather was cool enough to butcher hogs, nothing went to waste. The fat was used to make lard and the left over cracklings were used to make lye soap. The hog heads were boiled and used to make mincemeat for yummy mincemeat pies at holiday times.

On Saturdays after harvest, Zolie would load up the wagon with vegetables, meat, eggs and butter and barter them for items that they couldn't grow. On these outings Zolie would often treat Olie and OlaB to some candy or ice cream. This was a much-looked-forward-to experience for the children.

If anyone needed a doctor, the service fees were usually paid with a hog, a calf or some chickens. The bartering system was used to cover not only doctor's fees but many types other services as well.

During the second winter, Rosa had to go to Pittsburg to the doctor often. The Peters always drove her there in their car, it wasn't very fast but still a little faster than the wagon. Zolie would stay home and watch the children during these times when Rosa was away. When he had to attend to the farm, John would help out by staying and watching the children. Her illness extended into the early summer. One day when she had gone to the doctor, Zolie had to take the children with him to plant corn. He had only a few more rows to plant so he left Olie and OlaB at the end of a row under a shade tree. Olie saw some berries high up in the tree and climbed up and ate one or two of them. OlaB didn't eat any, but in just a little while Olie's face was thoroughly broken out and when Zolie saw Olie's face he *knew* what Olie had eaten. It was poison oak! Another lesson learned the hard way!!! Rosa continued going to the doctor for a throat condition, but the doctor never actually diagnosed what her trouble was.

The next winter, Zolie started studying the Bible more often and would read Old Testament accounts of Biblical characters to his family after supper each night. He began offering prayers of thanks before each meal. John Thomas and Bert ate their meals with the Edwards family. John said that he didn't believe in God. Zolie and John spent several hours in the evening that winter discussing and studying the Bible. John never expressed his views about God or the Bible to Olie or OlaB or mentioned them again to Zolie. Bert was, however, pleased with getting to hear the scriptures since he had never heard them read or explained before.

Chapter Eight

John Thomas had heard of a horse sale at a near-by farm and he and Zolie went to the sale hoping to find a couple of good horses that Zolie could train as a matched pair of work-horses. They found two mares that Zolie thought would work just fine so they bought them, hitched them to the back of the wagon and started toward home. One mare was almost totally black and the other was black with white stockings and a white flame down her face. The black mare was acting feisty as they rode home and Zolie knew that he would have quite a job getting her trained.

The next day when Zolie tried to put a bridle on her she became sullen. He tried several times to saddle her or put a harness on her but each time she would fall down, close her eyes, and play dead.

"Come on you ornery, good-for-nothing horse," Zolie shouted. "You're supposed to be broken, what's-the-matter-with you? Am I going to have to teach you some manners?"

Zolie filled her ear with water, but still she didn't move a muscle.

"I'll bet you do move," Zolie yelled and called to John as he picked up a long pole and climbed up on top of her.

Zolie was just about to whack the mare when John Thomas called out. "You can't hit her. You might skin her up!"

Zolie said. "You just watch! I own half of her and I am going to hit my half."

With this, the mare jumped up. And, after that incident Zolie was able to make a good work animal out of her.

*****

In the 1920's, neighbors lived far between one another in western Missouri. In addition to the Peters, the next closest neighbors were the Zellers who lived five miles farther down the road. The Zellers, who were from Germany, and the Edwards had become good friends. They had a young girl, Francine, about the same age as OlaB. Fredrick Zellers could speak fluent English but his much younger wife, Ursula, could speak only broken English. Rosa, although, had little trouble communicating with her.

One day around noontime, Mr. Peters drove to the Edwards' house to tell them that Ursula Zellers was very sick and that he had called an ambulance to take her to the hospital in Pittsburg. Mr. Peters said that the Zellers needed Zolie and Rosa at once and that he was heading back to the Zellers' house.

Zolie hitched up his fastest team to the 'spring wagon'. He and Rosa sat on the seat and Olie and OlaB rode in the small space at the back of the seat.

"Hold on tight cause we are in a rush," Zolie hurriedly shouted. "We're going to run the horses."

The horses, Snip and Captain, were the fastest horses around. The five miles to the Zellers' home was still a long way in a horse and buggy, even when running at a fast gallop. They were almost at the Zellers' farm when a large black ambulance approached from the rear. The team had already sensed the approaching vehicle when Zollie slowed and looked around. He pulled the buggy over to the side of the road and stopped. He got out of the buggy and began talking to the horses trying to keep them calm. After tying the horses to a fence post as far to the right side of the road as possible, he held the horses' bridles, began stroking their noses and continued talking to them in an attempt to soothe their nervous trembling. The horses had seen very few cars and nothing as big as an ambulance, but once it passed them they began to settle down.

Zolie and Rosa got to the Zellers' farm shortly after the ambulance had arrived. As they entered the house, they found Ursula in great pain and Fredrik trying to help her get dressed.

With great urgency, Fredrik said with a trembling voice. "We have something very important to ask the two of you. I don't know what is going to happen. If Ursula were to die, we would like to ask the two of you to raise Francine as your own."

"We will raise her along with Olie and OlaB," Rosa said and Zolie agreed.

When the ambulance left, Zolie and Rosa took the temporary addition to their family home with them. Francine sat between Olie and OlaB, clinging to both of their arms and sniffling softly, as they slowly rode back to the Edwards' farm.

On the ride back home, Rosa remembered the story that Ursula had told her shortly after they had met. Ursula told Rosa that when she was still living in Germany a priest had raped her and as the result she had become pregnant. Francine was not Fredrik's child but Fredrik, being an old friend of her family, agreed that he would marry Ursula. Both Fredrik and Ursula's families were wealthy so once married, Fredrik and Ursula moved to America to avoid vicious gossip.

Fredrik had thought that Ursula probably had appendicitis and if it had ruptured he realized that she might not make it through the operation. However, the appendectomy was successful and in a few weeks Ursula was back home. She continued to walk in a bent-over position for several more weeks. Once Ursula was up and moving around and able to look after the household, Zolie took Francine back home and Olie and OlaB no longer had a 'little sister', much to OlaB's dismay.

Chapter Nine

John Thomas and the Edwards family continued to break and train horses. Well, Zolie continued to break and train horses, John had very little dealings with the horses except to feed them and clean out their stalls. John helped Bert with the farming, but in the back of his mind, he was hoping to move to Pittsburg, Kansas. Farm life was not what he had envisioned it would be.

The horse business had proved to be profitable and Zolie was working long hours keeping the business going. The Edwards family soon got into a routine, Rosa would hitch one of the horses to the buggy and take Olie and OlaB to school in the mornings. On nice sunny days, after OlaB got older, she and Olie would walk the three miles back to home.

One day in late fall, Rosa hitched Snip to the buggy and headed to the school to pick up Olie and OlaB. Snip had a quiet and gentle disposition and they started home at a trot. A boy on horse-back started to pass the buggy and Rosa pulled on the reins to let him pass when Snip shot out like a bullet and was off running. Snip left the boy on horse-back far behind in the dust created by the buggy. The harder Rosa pulled of the reins the faster Snip would go. There was a sharp turn in the road up ahead and Rosa knew that they could not make the turn going so fast. Olie remembered hearing the men talk about Snip's funny habit.

"Let the reins go loose," Olie yelled.

"What do you mean, let the reins go loose," Rosa replied. "We have to slow down to make the curve up ahead."

While listening to Olie, Rosa accidentally loosened the reins a little and Snip began to slow down just in time for them to safely make the turn.

That evening when Zolie came in for supper Rosa met him at the door.

"The kids and I had quite a time coming home this afternoon," she hastily said when Zolie walked in the door. "Snip just about killed all of us! She almost ran us into the ditch. The harder I pulled on the reins to stop her the faster she would go."

"I told Mom to loosen up on the reins," Olie said.

"Whoever heard of loosening on the reins to stop a horse," Rosa questioned.

"Did another horse go past you?" Zolie asked.

"Well, yes, a boy on horse-back came up beside us to go around and I pulled back on her reins to let him pass," Rosa answered.

"That was the problem," Zolie said. "Before we bought Snip, she was trained to be a race horse. The former owners told me that she could not stand for another horse to move up beside her. If you pull back on the reins she will run. The harder you pull the faster she will go."

"Why in the world didn't you think to tell me this," Rosa loudly snipped, being more than a little irritated. "We could have easily wound up in the ditch, probably even turned over."

"I didn't think about telling you," Zolie said. "Snip is just like any other horse unless another horse tries to pass her. She would have been alright today if you had not pulled back on the reins, which was her signal to run…."

*****

That fall was an exciting time for Olie and OlaB. It began with the runaway buggy. A few days later an airplane had engine trouble while flying over the Edwards' farm. The plane made an emergency landing in a meadow near their house. Rosa went out to where the plane had landed to see if she could help the pilot. He was not hurt and Rosa offered him some food before he tried to repair his plane.

Word traveled like wildfire! People began to come by horseback, buggy, wagon, and on foot to see the plane. It was not every day that people saw an airplane up close. Someone came by the school where Olie and OlaB were and told the teacher. Consequently the teacher dismissed school early that day.

"I'm going to run home to see that plane," Olie said excitedly.

"I want to come too, I want to come too," OlaB cried out to Olie. "Wait for me!"

"Grab hold of my overalls and hang on," Olie shouted. "If you let go I will go off and leave you."

Olie started out dragging OlaB behind him. He was almost three years older than OlaB and could run much faster. After about a mile she could no longer keep up with Olie so he slowed down and helped her by carrying her on his back.

They got to their house and was able to meet the pilot. He let them look over the plane while explaining to Olie how the plane worked and they later watched him take off. Olie was especially smitten with the plane and the pilot.

Olie and OlaB thought that they really liked their young teacher because she had dismissed school when the plane had landed.

The teacher was 18 years old and had just graduated from the eighth grade. This was her first teaching assignment. Since it was the 'roaring twenties' and being young, she loved to go dancing and partying in the evenings. She would stay out late at night and would come to school the next day with a very irritable attitude.

One of her responsibilities was to arrive by 7 o'clock in the mornings and build a fire in the coal stove, making the room warm by 8 o'clock when the children arrived. She was often even late to open the schoolhouse door by eight much less being prepared to begin classes. Often, during the winter, the school room wasn't warm until closer to 10 o'clock. This would set the mood for her to become grouchy and take her feelings out on the children, especially the younger ones.

'Miss Grouch', as some of the older children had nick-named her, seemed to especially dislike OlaB and often singled her out for punishment. On one especially cold day OlaB told her that she needed to be excused to go to the 'out-house'. The teacher refused to let her go and told her that because she had disrupted class she could not eat her lunch that day, and told her to stay in her seat while the others ate. Everyone heard what the teacher had said to OlaB, so when the noon bell rang and the children got their lunch buckets, Olie got his and OlaB's and told OlaB to eat her lunch with him. After eating her lunch with Olie, she was still needing to go to the 'out-house', so she asked her teacher again but was told "no, you have to sit still and be quiet". OlaB could no longer wait, so shortly after lunch she wet her pants. The teacher made OlaB stand up in front of the class and by the coal stove to dry her clothes. OlaB was only in the second grade but this made a lasting impression on her as to how she viewed teachers. OlaB know that she no longer liked the young teacher. Olie didn't either.

The teacher, 'Miss Grouch', had a habit of dismissing school early. It was a very cold winter day and freezing outside. Olie and OlaB had no way to let their mom know that they were out early and the teacher would not let them stay inside until their mom got there so they started walking the 3-mile distance home.

Zolie had taken a load of corn to sell and was on his way home when he caught up with the children. He stopped the wagon for them to get on. Olie was able to get up on the wagon with no trouble but

OlaB couldn't make it. Zolie saw that something was wrong with her and helped her to climb up and then saw that her clothes were frozen. Zolie questioned Olie about what had happened to get her in her predicament and Olie told their dad the whole story. Zolie took off his warm coat and wrapped it around OlaB and made the horses run so he could get the children home quickly and to arrive there before it was time for Rosa to go after them at the school.

"Well, you young'uns will never have to go to that school again until the school board fires that teacher," Zolie quietly told the children. After several weeks, some school board members visited the Edwards' farm, asking why the children had not been attending school.

Zolie told them about the incident which had happened to OlaB and that his children would not attend that school as long as that teacher was there. The board members returned to the school and informed the teacher that the school would no longer need her services. There had also been several other parents complaining about mistreatment of their children.

*****

During the early spring, Zolie was helping Bert break ground for planting new crops. Zolie would take Olie with him since he was growing older and Zolie wanted to teach his son about farming. OlaB also wanted to be taken along on these outings. One evening she asked her pop if she could go with them because she thought that she could do anything that Olie could do and wanted to try it. He told her 'no', but the next morning he looked at OlaB's sad face and told her to get her coat and come along. She rode on the breaking plow in front of her pop and talked his ear off for a while! She soon began to get sleepy and Zolie told her to get down and walk for a while so she could wake up. After a short time, Zolie was not hearing her jabbering and looked for her. She was tangled up in the wheel that was under Zolie's seat and attached to the breaking plow. It had her foot caught in a twisted angle and she was knocked out. Zolie stopped the six horses that were pulling the plow, and got OlaB untangled and hurriedly ran with her to the house. After he and Rosa cleaned the mud off OlaB, and when they saw that nothing was broken, Rosa put OlaB to bed to rest until supper.

This ended OlaB's desire to be like her big brother for a while, and she relished the time of being spoiled for a couple of weeks. Soon after this she noticed she always looked like a boy. She had always worn Olie's hand-me-down clothes and Rosa thought it was time to make her some girl clothes. That was the end of OlaB's tom-boy shenanigans for the time being.

Chapter Ten

John's Move to Kansas—

After breakfast, Zolie went to the breaking corral just as John was finishing the morning feeding.

"Morning, John," Zolie greeted as he entered the corral.

"Good Morning, Zolie, there's something that I'd like to pass by you," John said, looking down at his feet. "We have been partners ever since we left eastern Arkansas, that's going on five to six years now."

"Sounds about right," Zolie replied, waiting for John to finish what he wanted to tell him.

"You've taught me a lot about farming and about the horse business," John said, slowly and somewhat hesitatingly, as he continued. "However, I don't think that I have been a very good student."

"You've been a good help to me and you have been a big help for Olie and OlaB with their studies," Zolie replied.

"I have been considering by options," John continued, now with less hesitation while looking straight on at Zolie. "I have decided that I am not cut out for all this hard work and definitely I am not cut out to be a farmer! I have decided to move to Pittsburg and open up a horse barn. I could get a large barn where I could stable, feed, and water people's horses while they are doing business in town. Most farmers can't get to town and do their business and back home in one day."

"When you move we'll have to sell off all the horses and divide the profits. I will probably sell the livestock and move my family to a smaller place," Zolie concluded. "Olie is now ten years old and he is a big help but he's not yet ready to break and train horses and I can't take care of this large of a place. Both Olie and OlaB have grown fond of the horses and they will be sorely disappointed when people start leading them off."

After John Thomas moved to Pittsburg, Zolie and his family soon moved to a smaller farm in Kansas. He was disappointed that John had dissolved their profitable partnership, but he was not surprised. He didn't blame John at all.

The new place was just over the state line into Kansas. Zolie had to let Bert, his farm-hand, go because he was not sure that there would be enough profit from the smaller place, to continue paying him. Now, Zolie was left to do the farming alone. Zolie's fame for breaking and training horses was well known all over western Missouri and eastern Kansas so he still tried to work with a few horses at a time with the help of Olie. Zolie had kept his two favorite horses, Captain and Snip, and he would tether the new horses to Snip. She was a big help too since she would bite them if they tried to run!

*****

At the new farm OlaB helped Rosa tend the chickens, making sure that all of the hens were in the hen house to roost by sundown. At times, one of the hens would fly up into a nearby tree to roost and OlaB would have to chase it down. If a hen was left out of the hen-house over-night it could possibly get caught by some wild animal and killed.

OlaB also helped Rosa raise a vegetable garden and she learned to prepare and cook the meals. Meat was not always on the menu, none of the Edwards family liked chicken very much, which was the only meat available year-round.

Early one sunny Saturday morning, Zolie hitched up the buggy and he and the family went to Pittsburg to visit John Thomas. It was in the early summer and John was now settled into a house near the eastern edge of Pittsburg. The house was located in front of a corral with a large barn at the back. Zollie had previously written John and told him that they would like to come for a visit and asked if he would have room in his 'horse hotel' for the horses. John wrote back and told Zolie that his stable business was very profitable and that he would be looking forward to their visit.

After the Edwards arrived and while the grown-ups visited John, Olie and OlaB explored the barn and marveled at the magnificent horses which were stabled there.

While the children were looking around, Olie spied a small house just outside the back door of John's main house and decided to explore it.

"OlaB, come here and see what I found," Olie excitedly whispered.

"What do you suppose it's for?" OlaB asked. "It looks like an outhouse, but where does the stuff go when you are finished?"

"I don't know, but this cord is there for some reason," Olie said while pulling the flush cord.

They both jumped back, afraid that they had broken something. They hurried out and closed the door and went inside where the adults were. When they got inside, John and Rosa were in the kitchen beginning to fix dinner and Zolie was standing in the door between the living-room and kitchen visiting with them. OlaB quietly went over to Rosa and whispered to her about what she and Olie had done. John overheard OlaB and said that they had not broken anything. He said that the little room was a toilet and when you finish, you pull the cord and everything is washed away with water. After that both Olie and OlaB had to try out the toilet several times.

Rosa helped John fix dinner or rather John helped Rosa. Rosa was not accustomed to a kitchen with running water and an ice-box cold enough to keep milk for days. John had bread wrapped in a paper bag and milk in a jar. Both Olie and OlaB were fascinated by the ice-box. However, they both commented that the bread and milk didn't taste like what they were accustomed to eating and drinking, and it wasn't as good as Mom's.

That was the first trip to visit John Thomas in Pittsburg that summer. That fall, John invited the Edwards' family to come and celebrate the holidays with him. When they arrived, John had his house decorated with shiny tinsel and green cedar boughs with red berries attached to them. He had started preparing a holiday dinner and Rosa helped him finish. John had fresh oranges and apples and a variety of nuts and candies. Olie and OlaB were not accustomed to candy from a store, the only candy they got at home was made by Rosa.

The Edwards' family enjoyed celebrating the holidays with John. He was like an uncle to Olie and OlaB. On the morning of the third day, Zolie and his family headed back home. The western sky was dark and Zolie wanted to get home before the bad weather commenced.

Chapter Eleven

Move to Nebraska—

After the move to Kansas, Zolie was restless, not knowing what he wanted to do. He had almost given up on the business of breaking and training horses. John Thomas was a lot more help than he had realized and now with Bert also gone, Zolie was left in a quandary. Out of habit, Zolie tried farming again although his heart was not in it. He had little hope that he could make enough profit to really support the four of them. The farm was simply not large enough. Rose was still having problems with her health, and at times she had trouble breathing. The doctor in Pittsburg had not been able to find what was causing her problem.

Before the corn harvest, Zolie would ride into town to catch up on all the news. In the mid-twenties most of the country was still living as though their prosperity would continue forever. This did not help Zollie's mood in the least. As was the custom, the men would congregate in front of the post office and discuss the news of the day. He over-heard two men talking about a job opening in Nebraska. Zolie walked up and began asking questions about the job. One of the men handed Zolie the advertisement and he read that a large dairy near Pratt City, Nebraska, needed a foreman and he noted that the pay looked good. Zolie hurried home with the news.

"I have some good news," Zolie excitedly said to Rosa when he got into the house, grabbing her and twirling her around. "Jim, I just heard about a good job as foreman of a large dairy in Nebraska. The pay is better than I could ever make here on the farm, even from a really good crop."

"Bud, you sound more excited than I have seen you lately," Rosa said. "Let's sit down and you tell me all you know about this job."

They discussed the advantages and disadvantages of a move to Nebraska. Zolie decided to write and inquire about the job and in two weeks he received a letter telling him that he had the job.

Zolie then decided to sell everything except his three favorite horses. OlaB was sad to see all the horses and cows led away. She was especially heartbroken when she had to say good-by to her cats and dogs. Olie was happy when he was told that 'John', his collie, could go with them.

After their sale, Zolie bought a new wagon and built an over-bed across it, which made the wagon six feet wide. He covered it with iron bars and a water-proof canvas. He also bought a tent and a coal-oil stove. All of their clothes and other possessions were packed in wooden boxes and placed in the bottom of the wagon under the wagon's extension. Beds were made on the wagon extension with OlaB's and Olie's beds near the front of the wagon. Zolie and Rosas' bed was near the rear of the wagon and a small trunk was placed at the head of their bed where some changes of clothes and toiletries were kept, along with Zolie's guns, which were always loaded.

With the money Zolie made from the sale of the livestock and the corn crop he believed that they could make it to Nebraska. The winter had been a bad one and there was snow still on the ground as they left the farm and headed to Pittsburg. The road was a river of mud and the horses had to work extra hard to pull the wagon. Zolie had to stop and let the horses rest several times so it took almost all day just to get to John Thomas' home in Pittsburg.

By the time he had unhitched the team at the Thomas barn, he realized that they were not going to make it to Nebraska in a wagon. They would have to sell everything and go by train. They stayed with John until Zolie could find suitable people to buy his prized horses. After two weeks everything was sold and the Edwards family was on their way again. Zolie took the money to the bank and exchanged it for one hundred and five hundred dollar bills and put them in a pouch that Rosa carried under her arm pined to her slip. Since the money was in large denominations, the pouch was not noticeable.

The collie, 'John', could not travel with them on the train so Olie had to teach his dog to eat for John Thomas. As his custom, the dog would not eat or drink unless one of the Edwards family would tell him it was okay to eat. John Thomas agreed to keep the dog and ship him to Olie as soon as they got settled in a house.

The train traveled from Pittsburg to Kansas City. There they would have to transfer to another train to take them to Omaha, Nebraska, were they would finally transfer to a train heading west that would pass through Pratt City.

Olie and OlaB were very excited to be riding on a train. They had never seen a train up close, much less ridden in one. However, the glamor soon faded as the hours and days passed. The train stopped at every town and while it was stopped, if you needed to use the restroom or buy some food, you had to get off and scurry back on board because the train didn't wait on anyone. Food and restrooms were not available on the train.

They had a several-hour-lay-over in both Kansas City and Omaha and Olie, being somewhat outgoing, took OlaB's hand and attempted to visit with the Red Caps. The Red caps in Omaha were not friendly and OlaB decided that they were stuck-up. Olie and OlaB had never seen black people before and didn't realize that they were not allowed to talk to the passengers.

Mr. Smith, owner of the dairy to which they were going was scheduled to meet the wagon and take the Edwards family to their new home. When the train dropped Zolie and his family off in Pratt City there was no one there to meet them. They had arrived several weeks earlier than they were expected since they were no longer travelling by wagon. Mr. Smith didn't have a phone and there was no way to contact him.

Pratt City was a small town. There was only one rooming house in town and it was full, no vacancy! Zolie searched everywhere in Pratt City and finally found a 'Bed and Breakfast Room 'n Board. It was expensive but Zolie had no choice but to pay the high price. The room was small and the owners seemed afraid of them because the Edwards seemed strange. There were only 2 beds so they all had to sleep in the same room. The bathroom was inside and they really enjoyed a good hot bath in an actual bathtub, a first for all of them. The landlady was very stingy, not cooking enough for a meal, certainly not like the meals which Rosa cooked.

Everyone was growing very restless when the rooming house sent word that a room was available. The room was large and the food was good and there was an abundance of it. Olie and OlaB could now venture outside so the days passed quickly. While waiting for Mr. Smith to arrive, Zolie became sick with pneumonia, which greatly frightened and concerned Rosa and the children. Rosa remembered how sick Zolie was while in Arkansas during the flu epidemic. Luckily, this time, the pneumonia was short lived. The Pratt City doctor treated Zolie and he recovered in just a few days.

Finally, Mr. Smith got there on the previously scheduled arrival day, not knowing that the Edwards family had arrived by train two weeks earlier. Mr. Smith picked them up and he drove them to a large farm house about a half-mile from the dairy. Mr. Smith had just recently purchased the house. It had eight bedrooms upstairs with three bedrooms downstairs. The kitchen was large and directly to one side of it, a door opened up into a 'cob' room. In the fall of the year when the field corn was gathered, they would back the corn wagon, full of corn, up to the outside of the room. Here the ears of field corn were shelled with a shelling machine into a large bin and the cobs were then tossed into the cob room. These cobs were used to make a fire for cooking and heating the house. This made a good hot fire but didn't last very long, therefore, this job kept OlaB busy bringing in baskets of cobs for cooking.

The house was furnished with stoves and a few bedsteads, plus a couple of rocking chairs for Zolie and Rosa. That was about all that was supplied; however, Zolie fashioned one of the large packing crates into a table, and one of the smaller boxes into a cook's table for Rosa to use when she prepared their meals. They found some nail kegs around the barn and used them as chairs around the table. Zolie had disassembled the lamp table, which he had made for the household to use while they were in Missouri, and shipped those pieces along with their lamp in one of the large packing crates. These items travelled with them on the train.

Soon after Rosa had unpacked the last packing crate, Mr. Smith appeared at the front door.

"I have several cows that are in the process of weening their calves," He announced. "I'll bring them by in the morning and put them in the barn yard."

"What do you want us to do with them?" Rosa asked. "Is that a part of my husband's job?"

"No," Mr. Smith explained. "Until they are weened I want to separate them from the milking cows. I would like for you to care for them and see that nothing goes wrong with the calves."

"Just how many cows do you want me to care for?" Rosa unenthusiastically asked.

"I have fifteen head that are still nursing calves," Mr. Smith answered. "You can keep the extra milk for your family. I also will bring a few laying hens. You can keep the eggs."

The next morning Mr. Smith delivered fifteen cows with calves and a dozen extra hens because his hen house was getting over crowded.

Chapter Twelve

Shortly after Zolie and Rosa got settled into their home in Nebraska, they became acquainted with Roger and Betty Stevenson, their closest neighbors who lived three miles down the road from them and toward Platt City. Roger farmed for Mr. Smith but didn't want anything more to do with the dairy or with Mr. Smith.

It didn't take Zolie long to understand why Roger didn't want to work at the dairy. Zolie quickly determined that Mr. Smith, his new employer, was not going to be a good boss. He knew that he would probably not be staying long as his dairy foreman, so for the time being, the Edwards would have to 'make do' with their situation until something else became available or some changes were made.

Roger Stevenson owned a car and picked Zolie up and drove him to work at the dairy every morning and he also drove Zolie back to do the evening milking. This routine irritated Mr. Smith greatly since this took Roger's time away from his farming duties.

In Rosa's new position of 'cow nurse', she was able to save all the cream, butter made from any extra cream, and eggs which the family could not use and she traded them for food when the weekly grocery truck came by their house. This practice worked out wonderfully for the family because this enabled them to save the money which they would have spent on groceries, thus saving of all Zolie's salary. Rosa felt very pleased that she was able to contribute to the families' finances.

After about a week, Zolie wrote John Thomas and asked him to ship Olie's collie dog, 'John', to their new address. But Zolie hadn't remembered that the dog wouldn't eat from anyone that he had not been told to eat from. So after the four-day train trip, Olie's dog was almost starved to death. Roger had taken Zolie to the train station to pick up 'John'. When the car pulled off the road onto the lane leading up the farm house, OlaB ran out to meet the car with Olie sprinting ahead of her.

"You're finally home," OlaB cried. "We've missed you 'John'."

"'John' I'm so glad you are now safe at home with us," Olie exclaimed as he and OlaB ran along-side the car.

'John' heard Olie's and OlaB's voices as they rushed out to meet the car. As soon as they had stopped, 'John' jumped out and ran to the children. He was very dirty and skinny, which caused OlaB to start crying. Olie immediately fed and bathed him and in a few days he was back to his playful self, making Olie especially happy and so thrilled to have his special and devoted friend, 'John' the collie, home again.

****

When Zolie got home on Sunday mornings after milking, he would call the children to sit down on the floor in front of him and he would read the Bible to them and Rosa. As was his custom, he read the accounts of the characters and events recorded in the Old Testament. After the Bible stories, Zolie would ask questions about the Bible passages that he had just read. He and Rosa would then sing songs of praise to God. Soon Olie and OlaB learned the songs and would join in with Zolie and Rosa. There were no close churches anywhere, so this became their church service. Olie and OlaB were taught not to lie and to leave other peoples' things alone. They were also taught to treat other people like they wanted to be treated. Their training also included teachings that God was to be believed and obeyed at all times. More importantly, after studying in the New Testament, they were instructed that when they were older they would need to be saved by obeying what the scriptures taught.

Zolie was not easily angered, but when he did get mad he was mad all over! Mr. Smith pushed and pushed and demanded more and more. He would yell and curse at Zolie and Zolie would just take it and go on doing his work. On one occasion; however, Mr. Smith was especially vulgar with his cursing aimed toward Zolie. Zolie was pitching hay with a pitch fork and began chasing after Mr. Smith with the fork held in his hand, cornering him in the barn. Mr. Smith began to beg Zolie not to kill him, so Zolie told him that he would let him go this time, but if he ever talked to him that way again he would not be so kind!

The Stevenson family soon became good friends and the two families would get together for Sunday dinners. One Sunday afternoon while the adults were visiting, Olie, OlaB, and the three Stevenson girls were out playing hide-and-seek. Olie decided to hide by climbing up in a peach tree. He saw a large peach, just out of his reach, so in reaching for it, he stretched and grabbed a small branch. Just as he did this, the small branch broke and Olie fell, landing on his arm. His forearm was broken and one of the bones had punctured through the skin, frightening the girls. All four girls began running around screaming and all of the parents came rushing out to see what had happened.

Once Rosa rushed to Olie she found him leaning up against the peach tree rocking back and forth, holding his broken arm and moaning. Rosa rushed to Olie, kissing his cheek and stroking his head and shoulders.

"Oh my, oh my, son, what have you done to yourself?" she cried, while wringing her hands and fearfully running in the opposite direction, not knowing what to do.

"OlaB, go catch up with your mom and stay with her while I go and call the doctor," Zolie said with a nervous trimer.

Since the doctor lived only a short distance away from the Stevenson's house, he arrived in just a few minutes. After examining Olie, the doctor told the family that he would have to break the twisted bones and reset them. This would require anesthesia, so they rushed Olie to the doctor's office in Platt City. After Olie's surgery the doctor turned his attention to Rosa, telling her he wanted to give her some medication to calm her nerves and that he wanted Zolie to bring her into his office the next day so he could examine her.

Rosa said, "Bud, I don't want to go to the doctor, but if you think it is best, I will."

"I'll take you to him in the morning after I finish with my milking chores," Zolie said. "I've already asked Betty if the young'uns could stay with her while Roger takes us to the doctor. She said 'yes', and we will drop them off at their house as we leave for the doctor's office. It shouldn't take us too long."

After examining Rosa the next day, the doctor told Zolie that it appeared to him that she was almost having a nervous breakdown. He prescribed some medication, which after taking it for a few days, Rosa seemed to be a calmer person. After a few more visits to the doctor, he discovered that Rosa and Zolie had wanted a larger family but that she had lost the last two pregnancies. He concluded that her nervous condition was possibly due to an imbalance of her hormones. He began treating Rosa and she soon began to feel and act like her old self again.

OlaB was eight years old and Rosa started giving her further guidance and instructions in taking care of a house and in cooking meals.

During the time Olie was recovering with his broken arm, the favorite past time for the young ones was to play upstairs in the empty unused rooms. There were many grand-daddy longlegs living there. Olie thought it would be lots of fun to capture them and scare OlaB with them. This was great fun for Olie until OlaB's screaming and running captured Zolie's attention one day. He immediately scolded Olie and took OlaB aside to show her how to handle the spiders without any fear since they weren't poisonous to people. This activity ended for Olie and he had to find other avenues for self-entertainment.

At this time Olie started doing exercises to increase the strength in his arm and he had also always dreamed of being a strong man. He soon started running up and down the road and in the surrounding fields. The love of being outdoors and building his muscles soon became his passion. Olie had decided that he could improve his muscle strength by putting two straight chairs a few feet apart with a broom handle between the chairs. He would then lie on his back and pull himself up repeatedly by using the broom handle. OlaB was enthralled with her brother's ingenuity and wanted to use his exercise apparatus also. After a few attempts, she decided that it was too difficult and she gave up, deciding it was not for girls.

Things at the dairy were getting bad again. Mr. Smith had forgotten his encounter with Zolie and the pitchfork. Zolie could see that his plan to leave was fast approaching. So, after work one evening, Roger drove Zolie into Platt City where Zolie bought his first automobile, a Ford Model T truck. He was able to pay cash for it and that was always a big point of pride for Zolie and Rosa.

Zolie had learned to drive tractors while working at the dairy but he had never driven an automobile. He joyously drove his new truck home. He had ridden with the doctor whom he had worked for while living in Arkansas and had carefully watched him drive, so he had confidence that he could handle driving the truck.

While still in town, Zolie bought lumber, nails, bars, canvas and other supplies which he needed to build a 'house' on the bed of the truck, fashioned after the cover on the wagon, which they used in their moves. Zolie and the rest of Edwards family were about to become hobos!

A hobo is different from a tramp or a beggar. A hobo works for what he gets and the other two do not. A hobo never goes with his hand out, he does not steal or hurt anyone. He is a nomad, he does not have a house for a home and likely does not want one.

Zolie drove up the lane to the house in his new truck. The look on his face was a smile as wide as the sun. Olie and OlaB were outside playing when they saw the truck coming toward the house. They wondered who was coming to visit in a brand new truck. As the truck approached the house they recognized their Pop was the one driving it and they both started running toward the truck laughing and yelling.

"Pop, what are you doing? Where did you get the truck? Tell us, tell us," Olie excitedly shouted.

"Can we ride in it, is it ours?" OlaB sang out.

Zolie exclaimed, "Yep, it is all ours, bought and paid for. Go get your Mom and show her what we have. We will be leaving soon so I want you to help Mom get things packed and ready. Olie, you can help me get the truck ready for travel."

Rosa came skipping down the porch steps drying her hands on her apron. "What a beautiful truck, Zolie, I think you found the perfect one for us."

Zolie did not let Mr. Smith know about his plans. He worked on the truck during the nights, using lanterns to see, and on Sundays. Rosa started packing things up and getting ready for the move. She kept a supply of non-perishable groceries bought ahead and packed. They used only what they had to have, everything else was placed in crates and trunks. Zolie and Rosa knew there would be times that they would have to camp away from a town, so they always kept a ten gallon milk can full of fresh water.

Soon, Mr. Smith payed Zolie all that he owed him, so as soon as Zolie hurried home, he said, "tonight is the night."

Zolie grabbed Rosa around the waist twirling her and dancing her around the kitchen. "Rosa we are finally going to get on the road again and out of Mr. Smith's cussedness and ranting and raving. I can't wait to finally be rid of him and able to get out of here."

Rosa was so excited but couldn't wait until morning to tell the kids the news so they awakened Olie and OlaB, "wake up, wake up, we are finally going to be leaving Nebraska. Pop is home now and he says it is time to go so we will go in the morning."

That night the Edwards slept in their truck and the next morning, as soon as the sun rose, they started out on their journey. Shortly, they ate a breakfast which Rosa had made the night before and packed into small syrup buckets. This was a fun treat for Olie and OlaB since they hadn't had breakfast-on-the-go in a long time. They were now on their way.

A few miles down the road, Zolie started laughing, "Jim, what do you think Mr. Smith is going to think when I don't show up for work this morning? How do you think he'll be acting when he realizes that he'll have to milk all of those cows himself? I would give a plug nickel to see the look on his face!"

Chapter Thirteen

On the Road—

Now, the Edwards destination was Kansas, *again*. OlaB rode in the front of the truck with Zolie and Rosa, and she often went to sleep with her head on Rosa's shoulder. Olie had decided to make his and his collie buddy's seats up against the cab of the truck. This way, Olie would have plenty of wiggle room to get on his knees and observe what was going on. It took a while for them to adjust to the idea of going at a faster speed than they were accustomed to in their old wagon. The maximum speed which the truck could go was 20 miles an hour over smooth roads and there were not many smooth roads. Most were either full of deep ruts or rocks.

OlaB was snoozing after lunch on their first day. The road was rough and bumpy and Zolie was attempting to miss as many of the rough spots and pot holes as he could. Zolie made a sudden jerk, tossing OlaB against Rosa as he dodged a series of rough spots. OlaB was suddenly jarred awake and being surprised and feeling anxious about riding in a truck, commented, "Pop, slow down, you are going way too fast!"

From Olie's place in the back of the truck, he had a good view of where they had been and he could keep in mind questions about the things which he saw to ask his Pop in the evenings. At times, all he could see was their trail of dust since most of the roads were dirt. Olie loved the travelling and was full of amazement and questions about the different places which they passed.

Olie's first thing to say when reaching a new destination was, "Pop, tell me all that you know about this place, things are different everywhere we go and I want to know all I can about them."

The Edwards would pull alongside the road to set up their camp in the early evenings when there was no city parks available. In the mid-late 1920's there were very few paved roads and travelers were scarce. Gas stations, stores and mechanics were few and far between. They were finding out that only the larger cities had any conveniences.

Zolie was very careful not to run low on fuel. When they passed through Platt City, Nebraska, they purchased two 10-gallon gas cans and some road maps.

Zolie told Olie. "We will need to be on the look-out for places to buy fuel, Son, so I'll put you in charge of the maps. I want you to locate places that will most likely have fuel and at every stop you will tell me where they are located so I can keep my eyes open for them. This is a big responsibility, Son, and I'm counting on you to keep me informed."

Olie was thrilled to have this job and said to Zolie, "Pop, I won't let you down, I'll always keep the maps with me in my overall pocket."

Rosa was very adept at fixing their meals whenever they stopped. She could do the laundry if they were needing things washed and if they were lucky enough to be near a river or creek.

"Olie, I need you to get buckets of water and bring them up here from the creek, we need clean water for me to cook with and do up the dishes and wash up before bedtime," Rosa said to him. "OlaB, I want you to gather some kindling for the fire."

This became their routine as long as they were travelling.

*****

After about a week, they arrived at the home of their friend, John Thomas, in Pittsburg, Kansas. After a few days of catching up with what John had been doing, Zolie went looking for a house for them to rent. He found a small farm with a small house on the outskirts of town. Olie and OlaB enrolled in school in the fall of the year. The school was located within walking distance from their house. Olie started as a 6th grader, and OlaB started as a 3rd grader. Their education had been spotty but they had learned life's lessons as they travelled. John Thomas had previously taught them to read and write. Zolie continued to read the newspaper and the Bible with them, having them read to him every other paragraph or so. Rosa was a good singer and she taught them spiritual songs and happy songs she had learned as a child.

Since there few trucks back in those days, Zolie was able to get many jobs hauling goods for people. He also got work on building one of the first paved highways in Pittsburg, Kansas. These jobs kept Zolie very busy but some of the hauling kept him away overnight. Rosa did not like being alone at night with the children so Zolie was able to rent a big dog for protection. It was an Airedale, named Maggie. She had a very bad temper, not liking anyone, but tolerated the family. Olie would have to take a long pole and scoot her food and water dishes up to her. Maggie also had to be chained to a post near their front door to keep her from running away.

Zolie came home late one night and noticed that Maggie, the Airedale, was not acting just right. He got up early the next morning, wanting to check on her. He noticed that she was shaking violently and her eyes were all matted. As she started toward Zolie, she jumped, breaking her chain.

"Run, hurry, make sure 'John' is in the house, hurry," Zolie shouted at Olie and OlaB, who had just jumped off the porch, being very anxious to know what was wrong with Maggie.

Olie and OlaB were yelling and screaming, being very frightened, as they all ran into the house and got the door closed just as Maggie hit the front door.

"Olie, hurry and shut in back door, we have to keep that dog out of the house," Zolie anxiously shouted.

Just as Olie got the door closed, Maggie made it to the back of the house and sat on the back porch by the water well. Zolie knew he could not handle her there because she was slobbering and acting crazed, so he decided Maggie must be rabid. He could not shoot her there because she was too close to the water well and Zolie was afraid that her blood might contaminate the water.

Zolie ran to the front door, opening it slightly, and yelled loudly to their nearest neighbor, who lived right across the road. "Come fast, I need help, hurry I need you now."

After hearing Zolie's cries for help, the neighbor, Mr. Johnson hurriedly arrived in his truck. After observing Maggie's condition, he got his gun and a rope from his pickup and, after several harrowing attempts, he and Zolie were able to trap her with the rope by throwing it over the clothes line, and shooting her dead.

Zolie and Rosa had not previously met their neighbors, the Johnsons, but after that incident, they became close friends, being very thrilled to have someone that they could count on if needed.

The incident with Maggie instilled a real fear in OlaB of dogs, something she had to contend with forever. Olie was older and therefore did not let the incident bother him, he just learned from it and grew to trust animals but to give them their space when they needed it.

At their new school they had to learn to adjust to different children's personalities and quirks. One day Olie had stayed home from school, not feeling well. That day, a boy about two years older than OlaB, started picking on her as they were walking home. He was calling her names as he pushed, pinched and shoved her all the way home, being a tough kid.

Just before OlaB got to her house, he shoved her down a deep ditch. OlaB finally was able to pull herself out and went home crying and telling Rosa what had happened to her. Olie was overhearing what his baby sister was saying, so when he got to school the next day he confronted the bully and gave him a piece of his mind.

Olie cornered the kid and told him. "Don't you ever lay a hand on OlaB again or I will 'clean your plow'. She is a girl and much smaller than you and she is my baby sister. If you ever need to pick on someone again, pick on me!"

Ever since he broke his arm in Nebraska, Olie was determined to buff up and become able to take care of himself and his sister. Olie was mild tempered and easily made friends, and he was able to size up a person and learn their true nature. He continued building his muscles using the exercises outlined in the books, that the doctor in Nebraska had given him to help him strengthen his broken arm. This, and his love of running fast made him a strong young man.

During the time they lived in Kansas, there was a Polish family living about a mile further down the road. The family consisted of the dad, mom and two grown sons. The parents spoke broken-English, however, the sons spoke English somewhat better. They were hard workers and very thrifty and had put all their money in the bank, $10,000. Back then, that was a good amount to have saved. The bank closed its doors and they lost all their savings, causing the dad to almost loose his mind, threating to take his own life. A few days after losing all of their savings, he visited Zolie, telling him how despondent he was, to the point of not wanting to go on living.

"You can make more money, but you can't get another life," Zolie told him. "When you are dead it will be for a long, long time. The next time, bury your money instead of putting it in a bank."

This simple explanation was all it took to convenience him to start over.

Life on the small farm was simple for Olie and OlaB. While playing at the back of the yard one day, they found a wagon wheel which was covered over with a patch of weeds. The axel had been driven into the ground and the wheel put back on top of it. It looked like it had been done by the previous owners of the farm because the rim was rusty and looked as if it had been there for a long time. After Olie got some of his Pop's wheel grease and cleaned it off, it made a great merry-go-around for them to play on. They continued being inventive, using things around the farm and making up games.

One day a pup wandered into the yard. She was fun to play with and they soon found out that she had a funny habit. One of the kids would playfully pinch her nose and she would not nip at that person but go on to someone else and nip them. The game became one of the neighborhood kids' favorite game. One would pinch the pup's nose, they all would jump on the merry-go-round and the pup would stand and watch it go by until her head was spinning and she would walk around drunk, trying to catch one of the other kids. They would laugh themselves silly until Zolie caught them at their game and told them to stop teasing the pup that way, because it was not kind to do mean things to anyone, not even an animal.

Not everything on the farm was fun and games. Pop called Olie and OlaB to him as he sat on the back porch steps.

He said. "Olie and OlaB, John is very sick and I am afraid he won't last long. He has something wrong with his tongue, he can't swallow and is slobbering a lot. I'm afraid it's what people call 'black tongue'. There is no treatment for it. I will put him in the shed out back and I'll feed him soft food and we will see if this heals him."

Olie was horrified at hearing that his best buddy, 'John' was so sick. "What can I do, Pop, he's mine, I want to help him too."

"You can look in on him regularly through the day." Zolie answered. "Just make sure he always has fresh water."

'John' didn't last much longer. Olie would go and sit with him and rub his head and talk to him. Back in those times, vets were not called on to treat pets, just for work animals. Everyone in the family mourned the death of 'John', but especially Olie. 'John' lasted nine days from the time he got sick but he was remembered always.

Chapter Fourteen

During his trips into town, Zolie often visited with his friend, John Thomas. On one such trip, John and Zolie went to John's barn to check on a new horse and found a transient asleep on a bale of hay. He had apparently been drinking heavily and was still sleeping it off. Zolie was able to arouse him enough to learn that his name was Dick. John and Zolie noticed that his dirty clothes had at one time been expensive. John felt sorry for him and brought him a strong cup of coffee, telling him that he could sleep in the barn for a few nights.

Once Dick sobered up, Zolie and John learned than Dick's last name was Cummins and that he was a well-educated man. John offered Dick a hot bath, a shave and a haircut and a hot meal. While Zolie was cutting Dick's hair, John went into town and bought him a change of clothing.

After eating, Dick told John and Zolie his life story. He had been a ship builder in Baltimore, Maryland, but was originally from Philadelphia, Pennsylvania. He had once had a home, a loving wife and a new-born son. Both his wife and his child died shortly after his child's birth. He was devastated by their deaths and began drinking to kill the pain. He had quit his job, not being able to concentrate on anything but the death of his family. After a few months he became a full-time transient by riding the rails, not knowing where the train was heading and not really caring. Zolie talked with Dick at length that evening and Dick listened with great concentration. After their lengthy conversation, Zolie offered Dick a home with the Edwards' family until he felt like moving on.

Dick was a city boy and knew nothing about country life. He was willing to learn and liked Olie and OlaB so they taught him how to tend the garden. After six weeks, Zolie convinced him that he should write his former boss and asked for his old job back. His former boss answered Dick's letter after only a few days, offering Dick his prior job and stating that he was very grateful that Dick was coming back into his employment.

"When I get back to my job I'll also look for you a job, Zolie," Dick promised when he left, this time riding the train as a paid passenger, using the money which Zolie had loaned to him. "I have a good idea what kind of work you can do, you seem to be very adaptable and able to do almost anything. You and your family have been so kind to me. I was orphaned when I was a young teen-ager and have never been treated as a family member by anyone before."

"Thanks, Dick," Zolie answered. "I know that you'll be good for the money which I loaned you. And, remember, you pay it back only when you can. I'd be really obliged if you could find me a job. It is getting harder and harder to keep food on the table around here."

In a few weeks after arriving back in Baltimore, Dick Cummins sent Zolie a package containing all the money which he had loaned him. A couple of months later, Dick wrote Zolie telling him that he had found him a job. Dick told Zolie that he would be working for a man by the name of Mr. Reynolds, who bought old furniture and restored it. He was in need of someone to go and pick up the furniture and deliver it to his shop.

Zolie, always being ready for a challenge and the opportunity to head to new territory, sold everything that he couldn't get on the truck and he and his family headed for Maryland.

Chapter Fifteen

The Move to Maryland—

Soon after Dick Cummings had left for Maryland, Zolie had started letting his hair and beard grow long. He was looking forward to the job that Dick had found for him. Zolie wanted to go through Tennessee on his way to Maryland to visit his relatives, whom he had not seen for several years. Zolie was a big tease and his plan was to pull a trick his relatives with his new appearance by dropping in on them unannounced, hoping that they would not recognize him. He soon began to look like a different person, almost like a lumber-jack with his very heavy, full, black beard.

The Edwards went through Arkansas first, visiting Rosa's family. Olie and OlaB had never met their aunts, uncles and cousins. It was a wonderful plan to get to meet and know their kinfolks. Olie and OlaB were thrilled to get to know Rosa's family.

From Arkansas the travelling Edwards went to Tennessee. There were many relatives still living around the large family farm home. As they came close, Zolie stopped the truck down the road from the house, leaving Rosa, Olie and OlaB in the truck. It was after supper-time when Zolie went to the front door and knocked. Aunt Clyde and Aunt Pearl came to the door holding a coal-oil lamp. They were surprised and frightened to see a stranger with long hair and a very long beard standing at the door and asking for something to eat and saying he hadn't eaten for two days.

Zolie's mother heard this 'stranger' saying that he and his family needed some food, so she said, "let that man in and get some food on the table. No one goes away from my house hungry."

Zolie was sitting at the table watching his mother as she was cooking her second supper that evening, since her family had already eaten.

In telling his 'big tale', Zollie said, "my wife and young'uns are outside, can I bring them in by the fire?"

His mother emphatically said, "yes, go get your family and bring them in here, they have to eat too and they are probably freezing out there."

Rosa, Olie and OlaB tried to act as though they were cold and hungry, the way Zolie had instructed them to act. Zolie's mother gave him the first plate of food and it was difficult to eat as though he was really hungry because they had also already had their supper. Zolie's mother was sitting with them and chatting and when she said something humorous, Rosa giggled. As soon as his mother heard Rosa, she remembered the sound of her voice, and looking over at Zolie, she finally recognized him by the sound of his voice and caught on to the trick Zolie was trying to pull. And, his mother almost beat Zolie to death for tricking her so badly, all the while hugging him to her breast and happily slapping him on his back.

For the next few days, Zolie and his family continued on to his brothers and sisters' homes trying to pull the same trick on all of them. It was a great two weeks, getting caught up on all his kinfolk's lives. There were many late nights, big suppers together, and lots of sharing their pasts, all laced with hugs and back slaps. It was an exciting time for Olie and OlaB because they finally had cousins, aunts, uncles and especially a grandma!

Leaving was a very tear-filled and emotional event. Looking back at his boy-hood home and seeing his aging mother, his brothers, sisters and their families was a heart wrenching time for Zolie, and Rosa, as well. They left with the desire to make that journey again.

Waving and shouting their good-byes, Zolie and Rosa cried. "We'll be back, we promise."

The family reunion was now over and they were on their way to Maryland. The weather was cold and rainy. Their days began as soon as it was light enough to drive and ended in the early afternoon, before dark. Since it was winter, there could be very little out-door cooking, so they tried to eat at least one meal a day in a café, if they could find one! Cafes were few and far between, with most located in private homes. Most eastern states had parks for travelers to spend the night. Most of them also had electric lights, running water, outdoor toilets and fire-wood.

The Edwards really missed their good home-cooked meals which Rosa was noted for. Most of the food they found in cafes was not what they were accustomed to, especially since they were seasoned somewhat differently.

Zolie quietly said one night as they were eating supper in a home-owned café. "Oh, what I wouldn't give for a bowl of beans. I'd be happy to give six bits for one."

A waitress was walking by and overheard what he'd said. In a few minutes, she brought out a family-sized bowl of beans.

"Sir, this is the bowl of beans you said you wished you had," the waitress said.

Zolie was astonished, but the entire family had all the beans they could eat that night. What a treat, the bowl of beans cost almost as much as the rest of their meal, but Zolie gladly paid the price.

Travelling over the Appalachian Mountains was quite a different experience than when they traveled from Nebraska to Kansas. There were not many roads that were paved. One evening as Zolie was driving on the bluff side of a steep incline, they reached the crest of the mountain, and as he started down, the clutch in the truck went out, sending them spiraling down the other side.

Zolie jerked the truck toward the mountain side, yelling, "I can't stop the truck, hurry, Olie, jump out and throw some of those big rocks under the wheels. Be careful, this might get really tough."

Olie did as his pop said and began picking up large rocks and throwing them under the back wheels. He was able to slow the truck down by lodging the rocks under the wheels enough so that it got stopped. Not having much in the way of tools, Zolie had to walk to the garage which they had just passed. It was a mile-hike back to get what he tools he needed. Zolie was able to fix most anything that went wrong with his truck, but since it was getting late and he needed to find a spot for the family to stop for the night, he paid a mechanic to help him fix it. This was an unusual thing for him to do since he prided himself on being able to fix almost anything.

The journey to Maryland had been a tiresome and long trip. Zolie only had the new boss's letter which contained the directions to locate his house. They turned off the main road onto a very narrow, winding, muddy lane. The lane threaded through tall trees which grew on each side, making a thick shadowy canopy. When they arrived near the end of the lane, it opened up into a large expanse of lawn. They made a left turn and followed a small graveled road past a large two-story house on their left. Just beyond it, stood a three-story mansion. Not knowing what to expect, they were very surprised to see such a beautiful place. They had followed the directions the boss had sent to them but they could hardly believe that something this beautiful could be the right place.

Chapter Sixteen

The directions in the letter from Mr. Reynolds mentioned that the house which was intended for them, was the third house down the gravel road. This was also a two-story house. According to Mr. Reynolds' letter, all three houses were built in the early 1800's. The house in which they were to live had modest furnishings but the up-stairs bedrooms were used to only store some of his period furniture and the letter stated that they were not to use these rooms. The Edwards did not have anything but the bare essentials which they had brought with them in Zolie's truck, subsequently, moving in did not take long.

As they were getting settled in, there was a knock on the front door. To their amazement, there stood a pleasant-looking black woman in her late thirties, smiling broadly, and holding a plate of home-made cookies.

"Welcome, you must be the new people that are here to help Mr. Reynolds with the furniture business," she said. "My name is Mary Johnson and I am Mr. Reynold's maid, cook and house-keeper. My 21-year-old son, Bill, and I live in the first house up the lane. Anything you need to know about this place, ask, I have lived here for quite a while!"

The things 'Miss Mary' told Rosa about Mr. Reynolds gave them a real insight as to his character. Miss Mary started by telling Rosa that Mr. Reynolds was very honest in his dealings with people, but he did have some strange and odd ways of behaving.

A few days later while Mary and Rosa were sitting on Mary's front portico shelling some peas, Mary told Rosa in her Southern drawl, "Mr. Reynolds was only married for a short time, it didn't work out, so he has lived alone for a long time now. He didn't even have a picture of his wife so he found a picture of a petty woman in a book, cut it out, framed it and said that that was his wife. It's been hanging in his bedroom ever since."

Mary continued her history of Mr. Reynolds with a bit of hostility, "You, know, Miss Edwards, I was just fifteen-years-old when I started working here for Doc Reynolds, Mr. Reynold's father. My son, Bill is also Mr. Reynold's son, although he does not acknowledge him. He does not even think that we're good enough to eat at his table or live in his house, but I was good enough to lay with him and have his child and raise him! He is good to us in his own way, but it only goes so far. You see, Doc Reynolds seemed to really like me and he left me enough money in a trust-fund to pay for taking care of Mr. Reynolds for as long as he lives. I'll show you his house someday when he is in town, it is quite—a place."

One night when Mary had finished cleaning and polishing the furniture in the 'Big House' she invited Rosa, Olie and OlaB to take a tour. All of the furniture was old and expensive and the house was kept just like it was when Dr. Reynolds had practiced medicine there over seventy years ago. His office was maintained just the way he left it when he died. The office was filled with jars and bottles of preserved specimens of body parts and animals.

Olie poked OlaB on the shoulder and said. "Take a look at all those body parts and animals in those jars, do you know what they all are? They look really interesting to me, I think I would like to learn more about them."

OlaB said shyly, "they look scary to me, Olie, I don't even want to look at them, let's leave this room."

The entire house had the appearance of a museum. The living room floor was covered with a red wool carpet and across from the entry stood a large grand piano. A spinning wheel sat to one side and a large fireplace was across from the piano. There was a settee and chairs around the piano. Tables and lamps were in abundance.

A large room with what seemed to be ten-foot ceilings extended across the front of the mansion and served as a ballroom and a place to entertain with dinner parties. The beautiful and ornate cabinets were filled with vintage wines and expensive china.

The second floor contained several bedrooms. The mansion was built prior to indoor plumbing so there were no indoor bathrooms in the house. 'Bed-chambers' were under the edge of each bed, as though some one would be spending the night.

After the tour Mary invited the Edwards over to her house to play cards. There was a bell affixed to her living room which was used by Mr. Reynolds to summon Mary when he needed her. Bill was a strong and handsome young man and was a hard worker, he was on call for two older women to drive them wherever they wanted to go and to do odd jobs around their houses. Card playing and visiting in Mary and Bills' home became a weekly outing for the Edwards. They became great friends and shared many good times together. Bill was delighted to have some children around and it became his custom to bring them ice cream, in small cups, a treat indeed for Olie and OlaB.

Dick Cummings was delighted that Zolie and his family were living close to him. At Christmas time that year, Dick caught a train and came to Zolie's home and brought Olie and OlaB lots of Christmas goodies. Rosa cooked a large and luscious Christmas dinner and insisted that he stay a few days so that they could get caught up on all that had been happening in his life. This was a very enjoyable time for all.

After Christmas break Olie and OlaB enrolled in school. The school was about a mile from their house. OlaB remembered her challenging school experiences in Kansas and wasn't very enthused about going to school at all. It was a two-room school house and a woman taught grades one through five in one of the rooms. She carried a ruler at all times. Anytime someone would do something she didn't like, she would whack their hand with the ruler. This didn't do anything to improve OlaB's interest in school. Olie attended school in the other room and was thrilled to be going to school again, always interested in learning something new.

Both OlaB and Olie had been accustomed to wearing overalls, but in the east all of the boys wore knee pants. Before arriving at the school building, a group of sixth-grade-boys began teasing and taunting both of them, especially Olie. They began pushing Olie and pulling at his overalls, laughing and making fun of him and OlaB. Olie had an eye for sizing up a person, even at his young age of twelve, and he soon located the leader of the gang of boys. Olie turned and tackled him, holding him down and hitting him, giving him a bloody nose. Luckily he had been building his strength ever since he broke his arm in Nebraska. After school that evening they told Rosa about the incident and she made them new clothes for the next day. Their new duds were made from cut-off overalls.

Later on, on February 12th, on Olie's thirteenth birthday, Dick Cummings came for a visit and Rosa cooked another big dinner. She invited Bill, Mary and Oscar Reynolds to come to join them for the birthday celebration dinner. Oscar said that he had a headache and couldn't come. Rosa fixed him a big plate of food and took it over to his house, which he ate heartily.

Later, Mary told Rosa, "Mr. Reynolds thinks that he is a 'Southern Gentleman' with his mustache and goatee and all his woman-chasing ways! He thought it was beneath him to eat with 'common folks' and that is why he said he had a headache."

"That is the last plate of food I'll take him and I'll never invite him in our home again." Rosa emphatically told Mary.

At the age of ten, OlaB began helping Rosa with the housework and cooking. OlaB was interested in learning how to cook and she had been watching Rosa cook for quite a while and understood most of what needed to be done.

Most days started with a wet fog, being so close to Chesapeake Bay. This was not good for Rosa's sinus condition. After a period of several days with no sun, she developed a sinus infection and lay down for a while with a hot pack on her face, so, OlaB was in charge of preparing supper that evening. When she would have a question, Rosa would tell her what to do. The bread was a little to brown and the beans were a little too salty, but everyone ate their fill and didn't make a fuss.

Dick Cummings convinced Zolie to take off a couple of days from work, he wanted to take the entire family to Atlantic City. So, early one morning everyone boarded an electric train in Baltimore and spent a day on the Boardwalk. There were bands and clowns and parades all morning.

Rosa had previously fixed a picnic lunch for all of them and after lunch Dick got OlaB and Rosa settled into a hotel with an ocean view. After getting them settled, Dick took Olie and Zolie to board the train bound for New York City to see a boxing match at Madison Square Garden. After they left the boxing match, they returned to Atlantic City, picked up Rosa and OlaB at the hotel and took a late-night train back to Baltimore. What a big day! That was the first time the Edwards had seen the ocean and the first time Olie and Zolie had visited New York City. It was a day that none of them ever forgot!

Chapter Seventeen

The Move to Flint Michigan—

When Zolie got to work a few days after returning from Atlantic City, Oscar Reynolds met him with the bad news that his bank was foreclosing on his furniture business. Oscar admitted to Zolie that for some time he had been dipping into the business accounts to support his playboy life-style and that he would now have to apply for bankruptcy. He told Zolie that he would have to sell all of the fine antique furniture that had belonged to Dr. Reynolds. The trust fund, set up by his father, wasn't large enough to support the business and also his extravagant way of living. Now, he was destined to live a modest existence.

"Gather around, I have some news to tell all of you," Zolie said as soon as he got home that evening. "Mr. Reynolds is going bankrupt and is going to have to sell all of the furniture to help pay off his creditors. I won't be working for him after the sale. I don't feel sorry for Mr. Reynolds but have told him that I will help him arrange for the sale. We will gather all the furniture which is stored upstairs in this house as well as all the furniture which is stored in other buildings located here on his property."

"What can I do to help, Zolie?" Rosa asked. "I can clean and polish all the furniture which has been stored and make it shine like new. This way he can make more money from it. After the sale, what are our plans?"

"I still have a job for the next two weeks while helping get things ready to sell," Zolie explained. "Mr. Reynolds just now asked me to see if you would help with the sale."

"I wouldn't have most of the pieces of furniture in a house of ours," Rosa said. "I have been upstairs looking around a little, and we don't want any of his things and I'll do all I can to help you, not him!"

"Just help him out as best you can," Zolie said. "I think he wants you to help make the furniture presentable."

After supper OlaB and Olie discussed the news they had heard. It was met with mixed emotions. Neither of them were pleased with the school in Maryland. OlaB disliked her teacher and also thought that the teacher disliked her. And, Olie had had a problem with some of the boys in his grade. Neither of them had made any close friends of their own age. The kids were just too different to what they were accustomed.

"I don't like to go to a new school and be the strange kid-on-the-block," OlaB said to Olie when they heard the news. "I guess we will be on the road again!"

"OlaB, don't talk like that," Olie said trying to make the best of the situation. "Just think of it as a new adventure. The ability to see new places."

"All of the kids think that we are strange," OlaB said sorrowfully. "I think that they are strange, only seven of my classmates are even allowed to say all of the Lord's Prayer in the mornings before class."

"I have to establish myself each time we go to a new school," Olie said. "I think part of our problem is that we usually talk like adults and we have been to a lot of different places. We will just have to make the best of the situation. Pop has to make a living for us and we need to support him by not grumbling."

*****

74

After hearing that the Reynold's furniture business was failing, Dick Cummings was beside himself. He knew that if Zolie couldn't find another job soon the Edwards family would be moving. He was determined to help Zolie find work. Dick had a cabin near the ocean where he spent a lot of his weekends. He invited the Edwards to use the cabin while he took his two-week's vacation to help Zolie look for work.

Mary and Bill Johnson came to the Edwards' home with a farewell dinner on the night before they were planning to leave. Mary had prepared some of the Edwards' favorites and they each wanted to say their good-byes and to share a final meal with them. Bill brought a doll, which he had previously won at a fair, for OlaB, and a pocket knife for Olie. OlaB and Olie were thrilled with their gifts and treasured them for years, but were very saddened to be leaving behind their very good friends.

The Edwards packed all of their belongings into their truck the next morning and headed for Mr. Dick's ocean cabin. Rosa was looking forward to the sunny ocean breeze, praying that it would relieve her sinus problems. Zolie and Dick Cummings spent the next two weeks looking everywhere for a job for Zolie. No job was found. The job market was slim and it was beginning to get much harder for anyone anywhere to find work of any kind.

"I'll write to my sister Kate," Rosa said. "Maybe jobs in Flint, Michigan, are easier to find."

In a few days, Kate answered Rosa's letter saying that the Chevrolet plant was hiring a few workers. The Edwards family were ready to head to Flint, Michigan, where Zolie had been promised a job.

Rosa said to Dick as she got into the truck to leave, "I'll give you my sister Kate's address to her boarding house in Flint, Michigan. This is where we will be while Zolie starts his job at the Chevrolet Plant. Please write to us so we can keep up with you."

"I'll write as soon as I can, I'll want to find out if Zolie got the job and how it is working out," Dick Cummings replied. "I will certainly miss all of you, especially those two rascals of yours, they have become like my own kin."

It was very difficult to say their good-byes to Dick since he had become like a close relative to them also. They had been at the boarding house for less than two weeks when they received a disturbing letter from some close friends of Dick Cummings, telling them that Dick had died suddenly from a ruptured appendix. The Edwards' address had been found in his wallet.

Chapter Eighteen

Move to St. Louis Missouri—

Rosa was surprised at the cool reception she received from her sister, Kate. Kate was two years older than Rosa but when they were growing up they more like friends than sisters, and they associated with the same group of friends. From the time Zolie and Rosa were married, they had not been close and had not kept in touch with each other. In Kate's letter, telling about the possibility of a job in the Chevrolet plant, she had not indicated anything to Rosa that she was unhappy with her. Kate had seemed happy that she had been able to help find Zolie a job. Therefore, Kate's reception had puzzled Rosa. After the Edwards family had settled into one of the rooms in Kate's rooming house, Rosa approached Kate in the sitting room.

"Kate, what's wrong?" Rosa began the conversation. "Have I or Zolie or one of our kids done something to upset you?"

"NO, Rosa, no one has said anything." Kate replied irritably. "Just forget about it. From what you said in your letter you make it a habit of moving around every few months. Your gypsy-life-style is just too much, I imagine it is your husband not being able to keep a job for very long. He seems like a misfit to me!"

"Are we going to be in your way?" Rosa asked. "We'll pay for our room. I'll help out, I can help cook."

"No, thanks," Kate replied coolly. "Your sister Ann helps me run the place."

The conversation soon ended with Kate admitting that she had seen Zolie first at that neighborhood party several years ago and wanted to be the one to marry Zolie and that she was still resentful of her. So she stormed out of the room in a jealous rage.

Rosa told Zolie about Kate's jealousy of him and they both agreed that they wouldn't stay in the rooming house any longer than necessary. They decided that they would buy one of the lots in a new housing development Zolie had recently heard about and temporarily pitch their tent on the lot. In order to buy a lot, the building code required the owners to build a house of a given value but most of the new owners built a garage and lived in it until their house construction was complete. Most of the owners were about the same age as Zolie and Rosa and were either living in a newly constructed garage or in tents. The Edwards family set up their tent on their lot and soon made several friends. All the young families met together and had a party at least once a week. Zolie's job was good and they planned to soon start building a garage.

It didn't take long for Rosa to see that her younger sister, Ann, was also unhappy living at the rooming house with Kate.

"Ann, come and live with us," Rosa said, one day when she and Ann were alone at the Edwards' tent. "I know that you are not happy there."

"I'm afraid to live in a tent," Ann replied. "I want a solid roof over my head."

"You know that you are always welcome," Rosa continued. "There is enough room."

"Thanks," Ann said. "I know that I would be welcome. You know Kate thinks that your family are all gypsies. I'm not sure that I would be comfortable moving around as much as you do."

"Ann, we work for everything we have," Rosa said, as Ann turned to leave.

When Zolie got home from work, Rosa related to him her conversation with Ann.

As he got a can of red paint, Zolie said, "I'll fix that!"

So he painted, 'HOBO' S HOME', across the front of their tent. Their friends had a good laugh out of the name.

Zolie had a good-paying job at the Chevrolet plant. He and Rosa finally felt secure. Olie and OlaB started to school and everything appeared to be working out. Then, Chevrolet sent a memo stating that they were going to have to lay off workers. Zolie was among the last to be hired so he was among the first to be laid off. Aside from the Chevrolet plant, there were not many other jobs to be found in Flint, Michigan. Every week additional layoffs were happening. Zolie knew that he would have to look elsewhere for work because all the jobs available were only for a few days and from time to time. Several of Zolie's brothers and their families had moved to Saint Louis, Missouri, and were all working.

Zolie loaded up the truck and he and his family were on their way to St. Louis, much to OlaB's dismay.

"Your grandma and several cousins live in St. Louis," Rosa said to help OlaB adjust to another move. "You will have a lot of fun and don't be bothering your Pop about this, he is upset enough as it is."

Grandma Edwards' health was failing so Raymond, Zolie's brother, had rented out the family farm in Tennessee and moved her to St. Louis so that they could help care for her. Zolie told Olie and OlaB that they would be living close to their Grandma and uncles and aunts and lots of cousins.

"Yea," cried OlaB. "I didn't know that we would have kids around. I guess we will be like other kids now. And, I know Olie and I will love being with Grandma. I remember how much fun we all had when we stopped by Grandma's house in Tennessee, unannounced. Remember, Pop that was the time you grew your hair and your beard long and tried to fool everyone that you were some stranger stopping by."

Olie and OlaB started to another school, which was only five blocks from their small rental house. This was a special treat because they could walk home for their lunch and eat Mom's cooking. One day before afternoon recess the teachers had passed out small flags to the school kids. The kids were so amazed to see Lindbergh's plane flying over the school. They waved the little flags at the plane and Lindberg dipped low enough that they could see him smiling down and waving back to them. What a memory.

Not all was fun and games, however. That year, Olie and OlaB got the mumps and measles and they had to stay in darkened rooms for almost 4 weeks. The world was changing—the big crash came. Every day the newspapers were full of accounts of men jumping out of high-rises or shooting themselves. Soon, there were very few jobs and if you could find one, the wages were so small that one could not live on the salaries. Zolie had previously been able to find a few odd jobs in St. Lewis but now there were definitely none to be found.

The kids and Rosa would see Zolie studying maps and walking around, slumped shouldered, with a far-away and sad look on his face.

Olie knew the signs by then, so, he talked to OlaB and said, "get yourself prepared, it won't be long and we will be on the road again!"

And sure enough, Olie and OlaB came home from school a few days later and saw the truck rigged and ready to go to places unknown!!! The good times with kinfolks were over. The night before they left everyone gathered to say good-bye.

Chapter Nineteen

Farm Labor circuit (year one)—

Springfield, Arkansas, was the home of a large research farm operated by the University of Arkansas. Zolie had heard about the research farm while living in St. Louis, so that was where he headed. When they arrived, they were told that there was no work at present but that they would be needing workers in April. Zolie was told that the farms in southern Louisiana were needing strawberry pickers so the Edwards family were on the road to Louisiana.

Zolie assured the harvest foreman that Olie and OlaB were responsible and old enough to pick. The foreman was not convinced to let children into the strawberry patch for his fear of possibly damaging the plants, but Zolie convinced him. So all four were hired. OlaB and Olie were thankful that their knowledge gained by working on the truck farm was now paying off. OlaB was small but she could keep up with the adults when it came to picking strawberries.

When they had finished picking strawberries in southern Louisiana, they followed the strawberry harvest until it was time to move to the Research Station in Arkansas. At the Research Station they continued harvesting strawberries. One day they got into a race to see who could pick the most berries. In four hours OlaB had picked 107 quarts and Rosa had picked 108. Zolie and Olie had picked a few more. The foreman was so impressed that he offered Zolie a job to work on the research farm. The position he offered Zolie included a house, so that ended Olie and OlaB's need to continue working. They started to school and were able to advance a full grade before the end of the school year.

The Research Station grew a variety of experimental crops and tested various fertilizers and sprays. Zolie was asked to keep a change of clothes in his locker so that he could change after applying some of the products. One day the foreman told Zolie that after he applied a new test product, that he should take a shower before changing into fresh clothing and that his old clothes were to be burned. Zolie carefully followed the foreman's instructions but that night he had a serious reaction. After midnight Zolie's face and arms started burning and blisters appeared, which soon formed sores, and also caused some of his hair to fall out. The next morning Rosa contacted the foreman who immediately took Zolie to the doctor.

After two weeks of rest and medication, Zolie recovered and his hair started to come back. Zolie was ready to go back to work but he decided that after his encounter with the spray, they would move on to follow the strawberry harvest into Missouri.

Most of the farms had showers and toilets for the workers and a place for them to cook their meals and pitch their tents. The 'Hobo's Home' got a good laugh wherever they went.

Once the strawberry harvest was finished, Zolie headed for western Oklahoma to sign on for the wheat harvest. A wheat harvest involves a long day's work. Work started at sun rise and lasted until sun set. Zolie was happy to sign on to a crew, but in the back of his mind he was always looking for a way to set down roots. The work was new to him but he was not afraid of hard work and caught on quickly.

The wheat farmer's wife prepared the meals for the workers. Rosa and OlaB volunteered to help with the preparation of the meals. Each day started before sun up with an early breakfast, usually eggs and sausage.

During the ten o'clock water break a snack was offered, usually some fruit. The noon meal was large and contained meat and vegetables. A mid-afternoon snack was available during the water break, then a final big meal after dark.

"Jim, after we finish the harvest on this farm, I think that it will be easier to be hired on the next farm if I can find two or three other men to travel with," Bud told Rosa. "I understand that the farmers send word to the next farm with recommendation of whom to hire."

"Bud, I hope you can find some men like Dick Cummins or John Thomas," Rosa said. "They became like family to us."

"I hope so," Zolie answered. "I surely hope so."

The next day during the morning break, Zolie was determined to make friends with two men that he had noticed were not involved in the 'foolishness' like the rest of the crew. One of them was tall with a slim build and had a Texas accent and the other wore a cowboy hat but didn't have a Texas accent. The code of the road was—that what a person wanted you to know they would tell you.

"How-ya-doing," Zolie said approaching the man without the Texas accent. "My name is Zolie Edwards and I am here with my family. My wife helps with the meals."

"You can call me Shorty," he told Zolie. "I have been working on a ranch in Montana but I wanted to see some of the country. Your wife is a real-l-l-l good cook. I have not left the table hungry. I am not married so home cooking tastes really good."

"I have noticed that you work hard," Zolie replied. "I have a truck and I think that we will have better luck at the next farm if we work as a team. What do you think?"

"I was hoping for something like that," Shorty replied. "I have worked on a ranch all my life but I don't know the ropes with this job. I'll be happy for a ride to the next farm and join your team."

Next, Zolie approached the man with the Texas accent. He had observed both men long enough to be able to size them up. The Texan told Zolie that people called him Slim. Both men were hard workers and neither bragged about what he had done or what he owned. Slim also agreed to be a part of the team.

Shorty and Slim were welcomed into the Edwards' family. They both liked Olie and OlaB and treated Rosa like a queen. They both had their bedrolls and were thankful to be able to sleep in the tent. They also both had been on the road long enough to have gained a lot of road smarts. The men told stories about often riding the rails. These stories reminded Olie and OlaB of their old friend, Dick Cummins, and how he and their Pop had become such good friends in Pittsburg, Kansas.

It often took a day or two to move from one farm to the next. Somewhere in western Nebraska, just as they were about to set up camp for the night, Zolie noticed what appeared to be a bad storm approaching from the west. They were miles from the nearest town so they hurried and set up camp just enough to cook a meal. Everyone scurried around to get everything put away, just as the storm hit. Slim and Shorty slept in the truck cab that night—or at least tried to sleep. It rained hard all night, accompanied by heavy winds and lots of lighting. Finally, morning came and Zolie was the first one up and began surveying the damage. During the night, a pack of dogs or wolves had raided their camp and had eaten or destroyed all of the food that had been placed under tarps for the night. There was no breakfast that morning!

Zolie drove until noon in search of a highway that would take them to a town. He finally found the highway, which was not much better that the muddy tracks that they had been following, but at least there were other travelers.

Not long after they were on the highway, they got stopped behind several stalled cars at the bottom of a steep mud-slick hill. Zolie surveyed the situation.

"The only way over the hill is for all of us to get behind the front car and push it over the hill, then get behind the next one and so on until we're all over the hill," he said.

While the men were busy pushing the cars over the hill, Rosa and OlaB began talking to a lady who lived on a ranch, ten miles on the other side of the hill. She was so glad to get her car unstuck and tried to get Zolie to let her fix dinner for his crew. Zolie thanked her but declined her offer, saying that they needed to get to the next farm as soon as possible.

The ranch woman, seeing the Maryland tags of Zolie's truck, said. "It's so nice to talk to people from a foreign country."

OlaB and Rosa had a good, but private, laugh after her comment.

Zolie knew that it would be late before they could get to the next town where there was a camp-ground. He had to stop to get gas and replace the food which had been devoured by the wolves. Every place where he stopped, would not sell food. In that part of the country merchants were not allowed to sell anything other than gasoline on a Sunday. Finally they arrived at a small town in South Dakota where a traveler's camp was located on the outskirts of town.

"Let me out near the center of town," Slim said. "I'll walk on and meet you at the camp.

Zolie, Shorty and Olie made camp and Zolie went around to the other campers, meeting them and telling them about their bad luck of losing all their food. He knew that everyone was facing hard times and he asked if anyone had some extra potatoes and beans that he could buy. Just as Zolie was getting back to his camp, several women from the camp started coming with their arms loaded with potatoes, bread, bacon and canned beans. Shorty started a fire and Rosa and OlaB started cooking. Before they finished cooking, Slim came into camp carrying two bags of groceries. After supper Zolie payed back all the groceries that the ladies had brought and thanked all of them for their generosity. That evening

Zolie made boxes to hold the food items which only human hands could open—animal proof.

The wheat harvest finished on a farm which was near the Canadian border and the Edwards family were soon to be on their way to the cotton fields of Texas. Shorty said that he would head home to Montana when Zolie and his family got ready to go to Texas. Zolie had previously left word with each of the farmers along the way that he would like to be on the crew for the next year and hoped that Shorty could meet them at the beginning of the wheat harvest.

The Edwards spent a few weeks working, doing odd jobs after the wheat harvest and waiting until the cotton picking in west Texas started. The camp had a long cook shack so Rosa had a field-day baking pies and cookies that she had not been able to cook over a campfire.

One day soon after the finish of the wheat harvest, Rosa was busily making some pies. A traveling salesman was also staying in the camp. He saw a good looking woman who was alone, making pies, so he brought his food to the same stove Rosa was using. It was a 'time-honored no-no' to crowd in on a stove that another person was using. There was another stove at the other end of the cook shack. However, the salesman took this opportunity to bump into Rosa and say suggestive things to her. Rosa called for Olie to come and stay with her until she could leave the cook house. OlaB followed. Rosa was still upset when Slim and Shorty came into their camp early that afternoon. The two men could see that something was wrong and when thy questioned Rosa she told them about the sleazy salesman.

A few minutes later, Slim and Shorty disappeared and in a little while the salesman was seen hurriedly throwing things into his car and leaving camp with a black eye and a bleeding nose. Luckily, the salesman was gone before Zolie got to camp that evening!

Soon it was time to head for Texas. Every one said their good-byes to Shorty and the Edwards were on the road again. Soon after arriving in Texas, Slim said that he wanted to go home for the winter so he would also be leaving. He thanked Zolie and Rosa for the friendship and hospitality which they had shown to him. He then said good-bye to Olie and OlaB. OlaB was saddened to have to say good-bye. She wished that she could have a house and friends. In the back of Zolie's mind, he still wanted to settle down on a farm of his own. He planned to do just that—one of these days.

Chapter Twenty

OlaB was especially saddened after having to say good-bye to both Slim and Shorty. She was feeling very lonely and a bit sorry for herself. After saying good-bye to Slim, the road to the cotton fields seemed especially long and dreary. Her spirits lightened a bit as the truck approached the farm because she knew that she needed to be ready to pick cotton.

"I don't know how to pick cotton," OlaB mumbled, just above a whisper.

"What did you say?" Zolie asked. "Speak up."

"How do you pick cotton?" she asked. "We have never picked cotton before."

"I have, it's easy," Rosa answered, trying to make a game out of the work. "You pick the white fluffy cotton and put it into a bag that you pull behind you. You will catch-on and soon be able to pick as much as me. Then we can run a race like we did picking strawberries."

The farm to which they were heading provided tents equipped with wood flooring for the workers. Each tent came equipped with a four burner coal-oil stove and an attached oven at the side of the cook-top. The truck was still used as the sleeping quarters. The camp was not equipped with a bath-house, so OlaB and Rosa didn't think bathing in the tent was much fun.

All four family members were able to work picking cotton. The Edwards were eating well and saving a lot of money. Their banking practice still consisted of a money pouch nestled under Rosa's arm and pinned to her slip. Banks were considered unsafe and few farmworkers used them.

Cotton picking soon came to an end and much to OlaB's dismay they were on the road again heading nowhere in particular. There was no harvest to go to until spring and for the first time they didn't have a house to live in during the winter. It was in December and the weather was getting colder. The west Texas winds would soon be blowing from the north and carrying half of Kansas with it along with sleet and freezing rain. Zolie wanted to get as far south as he could before all of the bad weather set in.

The strawberries in Louisiana wouldn't be ready until spring but Zolie loaded the truck and headed south. From where they were located in west Texas there were no roads connecting them to the highway going to Louisiana. So, Zolie used a ranch road and cut across a large ranch in an attempt to reach the highway. The road came to a creek that had just a little water in it. It appeared that cars and trucks had previously crossed the low-water crossing so Zolie decided to try. He drove into the low-water crossing and half way across he decided that he needed a lower gear. While changing gears, the loaded truck began sinking in quicksand. They were axel deep and decided to wade out of the water and see what could be done.

OlaB began to cry frantically and asked. "What are we going to do? Is the truck going to sink out of sight? We will lose everything!"

"I can look around for some limbs and brush to put under the back wheels," Olie suggested.

No sooner than Olie had made his suggestion, a truck load of cowboys came by and gunned their truck and made it across the creek and over to the other side without any trouble. Once across, they stopped and surveyed the Edwards' situation.

"Looks like you folks might need some help," one of the cowboys said.

"I think we do," Zolie said. "I thought that I could make it without shifting into a low gear, but I was wrong."

"Buck, take the truck and go back to the ranch house and get some long planks and a chain," the cowboy in charge of the crew said. "We'll get you all un-suck in no time."

Soon Buck returned with several long planks and a chain.

"Now, Buck, hook that chain to the front of their truck and pull up the slack," the crew chief said. "The rest of you put one end of the planks under the back wheels and sit on the other end. Now, Buck, start pulling and ease their truck out of the quicksand."

Zolie thanked them for all of their help and soon the Edwards were on their way again. After a few more problems of getting over some sand hills, they finally reached the road that Zolie was looking for.

They were near Amarillo, Texas, and Zolie didn't want to be on the road if a winter storm hit, so he decided to find a camp-ground and stay for a few days. It was December 24.

After setting up camp, OlaB pulled Olie aside.

"What are we going to do?" OlaB whispered to Olie. "Always on Christmas-Eve Pop would tell us to get a large box and put it in the kitchen, but we're not in a house this year, we don't even have a kitchen."

"I don't know," Olie whispered back to her. "We are older and maybe Pop thinks we are too old for Christmas. We are not making any money now, not since we stopped picking cotton. And anyway, when has he had time to go to a store and buy anything?"

"It's early but I think that I will go on to bed, OlaB said, leaving Olie and starting to sob as she climbed up into the back of the truck."

"Me to," Olie said sadly, as he also started for bed.

Both kids slept late the next morning, knowing that there was no hurry, and Zolie let them sleep-in.

"I need some things out of the cab of the truck, young'uns," Zolie said when the family finished eating breakfast the next morning. "There's too much for one, so you both need to go."

When Olie and OlaB opened the truck cab they saw two bushel baskets piled full of goodies. They saw a baked ham with all the trimmings, along with nuts and fruit, the ones they only had during the holidays. Olie soon reasoned that his Pop had gotten a ride into town after he and OlaB had gone to sleep the night before.

Zolie also got a gift, he bought the family a new truck. The new Chevrolet truck was much bigger and had lights so that they could travel at night. The Chevrolet had windows in the doors, not like the canvas coverings on the Ford. The whole family was delighted with this new truck.

Chapter Twenty One

Farm Circuit, Year Two—

Early the next spring, Zolie proudly drove his new truck to Louisiana to begin the spring strawberry harvest. It was getting harder and harder for people to find work of any kind. Since Zolie and the entire family had worked the previous year, they were given hiring preference and soon began working the harvest. Wages were very low, a person could work all day and make only fifty cents. People were extremely fortunate to find work. For every job, there were several people waiting to be hired so there was no negotiation over wages. Times were getting worse by the day. Everyone had to protect their own property because law enforcement, what little there was of it, didn't want to venture into the farm camps. Zolie kept his six-shooter under his pillow at night and wasn't afraid to use it. He also established a pass word at each camp, to be used by the family members when they had been away and then returned to camp.

Olie felt that he was as grown at age fifteen, so after a day of picking strawberries, he and a few of the other boys from the camp would go into town. They would get paid after work each day in nickels. One of the boys felt so proud of his earnings that he jingled the coins, flaunting his hand full of nickels as they walked into town.

One day a group of robbers were lying-in-wait outside the camp gate waiting to take money from some of the workers as they left for town. At first, they were not interested in a small group of young boys, but the jingling of the nickels got their attention as the boys passed by and they went in pursuit of them. Olie and the other boys began running and were able to out run the hoodlums.

On the way back to the camp, Olie separated from the others to take a short-cut across a field nearer to his camp site. Half way across the field, Olie noticed three men following him. They were shouting and talking about him flaunting his money.

"That wasn't me," Olie yelled at them and began to run in the direction of his camp. "I don't have but four nickels left."

Olie was able to out run the men and made it to the Edwards' camp. In his rush to get back to camp, he realized that he had forgotten to say the pass word. At that moment, he saw his Pop rise up in the dark with his six-gun aimed right between his eyes. Olie had to do some fast talking to convince Zolie that it was him before Zolie could get a shot off. After that, Olie never again forgot to say the pass word when entering their camp.

The strawberry season was now over and the early wheat harvest would soon be starting. OlaB was disappointed when they got to the first camp and Slim and Shorty didn't show up. Zolie had worked for this farmer the past year and he knew the kind of work Zolie did, so Zolie had no trouble getting hired.

"I am getting bored sitting around camp all day," Olie said one evening soon after the start of the harvest. "I help out in the cook house as much as I can but it is embarrassing to be seen chopping vegetables and gathering the garden. Pop, would you ask the foreman to hire me?"

"I'll talk to him tomorrow," Zolie proudly answered.

The next morning Olie reminded his Pop to ask the foreman. The foreman said that he could use Olie, so the next day Olie went to work with Zolie. The foreman tossed a shovel at Olie and told him to shovel grain until noon time.

"Olie, go back to camp and eat there," his Pop said when the workers finally stopped for dinner.

As Olie was leaving, the foreman stopped Olie and said. "You worked like a man, so you'll eat with the men."

That began Olie's working career. Even though he was dead tired that evening, he didn't say a word, but shortly after supper he went straight to bed with a great feeling of finally being treated like one of the men.

Not long after Olie started working as part of the harvesting crew, they finished the work on that farm and moved to the next one. That farm had a cook's house with a garden planted in the back. Rosa was hired as the camp cook and OlaB was assigned to be her assistant. It was all that the two of them could do to keep up with the meals. They started fixing breakfast two hours before sun-up and didn't finish supper until well after dark.

The harvest workers would gather at tables set up in front of the cook's house before sun-up and drink coffee until breakfast was ready. One noon, a few days after starting to work on the second farm, one of the workers didn't leave for the wheat field after dinner. He stayed back and after Zolie and Olie left, he came into the cook house and stood over in the corner behind the stove. There wasn't a lot of light in the corner so he was hidden.

Rosa was busy working at the counter peeling potatoes and had her back to the stove. She had sent OlaB out to the garden to pick green beans and snap them in the shade of a tree beside the garden.

Rosa finished peeling potatoes and turned to put them on the stove when the worker came up behind her and put his arms around her waist and began fondling her. He pulled her up as close against him as he could.

There was a large iron skillet drying on the stove that she had used to fry bacon that morning. She grabbed the skillet and swung it over her shoulder as hard as she could, hitting the man in the right temple. He was out cold immediately and fell backward landing on his left side. Rosa had to step over him to get to the stove but she was determined not to move him until someone came to get rid of him.

After a short time the foreman came looking for him and found him still out cold on the floor. He asked Rosa what had happened and she told him about the entire episode. OlaB was still out under the shade tree snapping green beans, unaware of what had happened in the kitchen.

The foreman left and soon returned with his wife and oldest son. They managed to get the unconscious man in the back of the foreman's truck and off to the nearest doctor. The man never showed up for work the next morning!

Zolie was getting 'itchy-feet' again to see new country, so after the work on the last farm was finished, they followed the western wheat harvest ending in Montana, near the Canadian border. The wheat harvest season ended early that year and Zolie was trying to figure out something to do before the cotton was ready to pick in Texas. He talked with several of the workers but no one had any plans about what to do until he met John Adams.

After talking to John for a while, Zolie learned that John was a rancher from Kansas. His family had remained in Kansas tending his ranch and since his children were almost grown they were able to take care of the ranch and the crop of broom corn until harvest time. He thought that he could make some extra money following the wheat harvest. He asked Zolie if he would like to come to Kansas and help with harvesting his broom corn when it was ready for harvesting. John admitted to Zolie that he had never grown broom corn before and Zolie said that he had never harvested broom corn before.

The day after the Montana wheat harvest finished, the wheat farmer's oldest son, Jim, who was Olie's age, came into camp. Jim saw Olie, and being the only other young person within fifty miles, came over to the Edwards' camp to get acquainted. After Jim and Olie got to know each other, and Olie then had time to kill before leaving for the cotton harvest, he and OlaB spent some time with Jim before closing up camp for that season.

The camp was located near the wheat farmer's fruit orchard. The farmer had recently purchased a new breed of sheep and had put them in the fenced orchard. His son, Jim, was excited to have some other kids to talk to so Jim took them to the orchard, which seemed to be a perfect spot to hang-out.

Jim introduced Olie and OlaB to the game of 'Sheep Tag'. Olie and OlaB didn't know that rams were dangerous and if given a chance, they would butt you to death if they got you cornered. The kids would antagonize the rams by running along the fence until a ram noticed one of them. Then, that person would run while the other two slipped under the fence and then run for a tree. This would draw the ram's attention and while the rams were chasing them, the other kid would slip under the fence and head for a tree. To get back under the fence and to safety they would have to go through the process again. This game only lasted for a day and was a great deal of fun, but Olie and OlaB were needed to help Zolie and Rosa break camp.

"It's too early for the cotton to be ready," Olie said with exasperation. "What are we going to do?"

"I have been talking to John Adams," Zolie answered. We are going to follow him to his ranch in Kansas. He has several acers of broom corn to harvest.

"What's broom corn?" OlaB asked. "Can you eat it?"

"I'm not sure," Zolie replied. "But if it grows we can harvest it."

Zolie followed John to his ranch. The broom corn patch was located in a pasture, almost out of sight of their house. John hired Rosa and OlaB to be the cooks for Zolie, Olie and the four other cutters. The cookhouse was a covered wagon with chuck boxes like ranchers used on a cattle drive. John had dug deep holes for the wagon wheels to drop down into so the wagon would not be so hard to climb into. In the back of the wagon there was room for a table and chairs. Water had to be carried from the farm house in ten-gallon-cream-cans and left in the shade of a lean-to-tarp attached to the wagon. Rosa and OlaB got up at five in the morning to fix biscuits in the one burner oven. It was just like what they used during the wheat harvest but a little more primitive.

While there, in the afternoons, Rosa had a little time to sew patches on the work clothes. Many people's clothes were ragged and no one had money to buy anything new.

"A patch by a patch is neighborly and a patch on a patch is beggarly," Rosa would say as she patched Olie and Zolie's work clothes.

"I am very lonesome out here," OlaB said. "It is so lonely! The only other things out here are cattle, goat heads, and sand burrs. When can we go back to the ranch house to get water? At least we could talk with the ranch women. I think that they are as lonely as we are. The only thing between us and the north pole is a barbed wire fence!"

"We will be leaving for the Texas cotton fields soon," Rosa assured her.

"We seem to never get to go back to places where we have been and see people that we know," OlaB said with dismay and a loud sigh.

Soon the broom corn harvest was over and the Edwards' clan said their good-byes to the Adams family and were on their way to Texas, again!

"That was quite an experience," Zolie said. "I am not sure that I want to harvest broom corn ever again."

"I am not sure that I will plant broom corn ever again," John added. "I think that I will stick to cattle."

Zolie and his family finally arrived at the Purnell farm in Texas. The Purnell's had two sons near Olie's age who also helped to pick the cotton. The Purnell's treated the Edwards like family. The cotton crop was good and the Purnell's and Edwards' were able to put some money away. In the back of Zolie's mind he dreamed of owning his own farm and not having to always have to work for someone else.

After the cotton season ended, Zolie decided to spend the winter in south Texas near the Mexico border.

"The weather is warm and things grow all winter," Zolie told the family. "We should be able to find winter work there."

"What's south Texas like?" Olie asked.

"I'm not sure," Zolie replied. "I think that they grow oranges there."

"How much farther?" OlaB asked after they had traveled several hundred miles through nothing but baron waste land and scrub brush.

Much to all of their surprise, as they toped a hill and started down into a valley, they saw a beautiful scene. Flowers were growing everywhere. There were orange trees full of fruit and vegetables were ready to be picked. But there were hundreds of people there all lined up looking for work. The dampness was already causing Rosa's head to throb. After two weeks, Zolie decided that they were not going to get work because they were too far down the list so they headed for Louisiana to spend the winter near the farm where they would start the strawberry harvest in just a few more weeks.

Chapter Twenty Two

Farm Circuit, Year Three—

When the strawberry harvest had finished, Zolie headed for western Oklahoma to start working in the wheat harvest. Since he never liked going the same way two years in a row, this year he decided to head farther west, to work in Kansas and Colorado.

After finishing a harvest near the foothills of the Rocky Mountains, Zolie stood in the shadow of the foothills and took his hat off and wiped his brow.

"We have never crossed those mountains," Zolie said while he and Olie stood looking at the mountains looming in front of them. "I think that I would like to try harvesting wheat on the other side. I heard that there is wheat to be harvested over there."

"Oh, good, I like seeing new country," Olie responded.

That evening, rather than loading up the truck and heading to the next farm to the north, the Edwards family headed west. It was July when they started up the grade and into the mountains. The road was narrow and winding, and it was difficult to see around the blind corners. At times, Olie would get out and direct Zolie round a bend on the 'one-lane road'. Luckily there was never much traffic.

"My nose is starting to bleed," OlaB cried, suddenly.

"Zolie, stop and let OlaB walk around for a while until her nose is stops bleeding," Rosa anxiously said.

"I'll stop as soon as I can find a place in the road straight and wide enough to stop," Zolie replied. "This will also give the truck a little time to cool off."

Shortly after stopping, OlaB's nose bleed was forgotten. She and Olie made snowballs from a snow bank left from the winter snow. Everyone was feeling a little out of breath and light-headed at the high elevation but the cool air helped revive everyone.

The road got steeper as they neared the top of the pass and the 'one-lane' got even narrower. The going was slow but Olie still had trouble holding onto the truck when it made one after another of the hair-pin-turns near the top of the pass. The tires pushed gravel off what looked like a thousand foot drop. Suddenly, the right rear tire fell into a hole up to the axel. The sudden jolt threw Olie off the back of the truck.

The jolt stopped the truck in its tracks. Zolie got out to see what damage was done to the truck, fearing that the axel was possibly damaged.

"Olie, come and help me," Zolie yelled, but there was no reply. "Olie."

Zolie called again and again but Olie didn't answer. Zolie looked at the wheel lodged in the hole and saw Olie lying unconscious on a rock ledge a few feet below the road.

"I need some help, Zolie cried out. "The jolt has knocked Olie over the edge. Hurry, bring me a rope."

Rosa and OlaB got a rope and hurried back to where Zolie stood. Zolie tied the rope around a bolder and the other end around his waist.

"I'm going down and tie this rope under Olie's arms and the two of you pull him up," Zolie said. "Then send the rope down for me and I'll climb up."

After several minutes, Rosa and OlaB had Olie up and lying on the gravel road. He was still unconscious but he soon began moving slowly.

Rosa looked him over and noticed a large gash on the back of his head. It was bleeding a small amount but began to stop when Rosa applied pressure with a towel.

OlaB looked down the road and saw another truck coming up behind them. The truck stopped and two men jumped out.

"What happened?" one of the men asked.

"I hit some loose gravel and part of the road gave way," Zolie answered. My boy was riding on the back and was jarred off. He fell over the edge of the road."

One of the men got into his truck and eased up behind Zolie's truck with the other man looking on to see if the bumpers matched.

"Ease forward," the man said. "Easy does it. Give it a little gas. You are about out of the hole."

A few minutes later Zolie was back on the road. He had looked at the wheel and decided that it appeared that no damage to speak of was done. Rosa laid Olie across OlaB's and her laps with his feet over in Zolie's lap. Soon they reached the top of the pass and stopped to thank the good Samaritans for all of their help. They rested for a while to let the truck cool off some and to let Zolie's nerves settle down a little. Olie began to stir a bit so Rosa lifted the towel to see if the bleeding had stopped. Olie began to sit up and in no time he was up walking around as though nothing had happened.

"The view from up here is breathtaking," Rosa said, not being able to take it all in after all that had just taken place. "Looking out toward the west looks like an ocean of blue. Do you suppose going down this side will be as hard as climbing up?"

"Going down will be hard on the brakes," Zolie said, remembering their trip to Baltimore. "The Appalachian Mountains are small in comparison to these."

Zolie found the wheat farm that he was looking for and spent the rest of the summer harvesting wheat in western Colorado near the Utah border. Olie stayed in camp for a few days before he joined Zolie.

*****

Delia, Rosa's sister, had married her husband, Albert, and they had moved to Utah many years ago and Rosa had not seen her for over twenty-five years. After the harvest, Rosa wanted to stop in Sandy, Utah, and visit Delia. The Edwards arrived at Albert and Delia's house, outside of Sandy, Utah, early one afternoon, unannounced. Delia and Rosa had a joyous reunion lasting well into the night. Rosa's sister and her husband had eleven children but only five were still living at home. Three of them were near Olie and OlaB's ages. OlaB was delighted to have cousins her own age to visit with. They spent hours comparing their lives and experiences with each other.

OlaB and Olie could read quite well but they were behind in their schooling in other areas. OlaB's cousins were two grades ahead of her so she decided to move herself up to the same grade as her cousins when she enrolled in school in the fall. One day when Rosa wasn't looking, OlaB got her report cards and burned them. With that, OlaB advanced two grades. That fall when the school officials asked to see her report cards when she registered, OlaB told them that her report cards had been burned. So, she was enrolled in the same grade as her cousins.

It was over a month before school started and Zolie started looking for some farm crops which needed picking. He quickly found a job working on a Utah Senator's farm since his cherry orchard was more than ready to be picked. Luckily, the Senator's crop was a little late. Zolie had never picked cherries before but he was confident that he and the family could learn quickly, remembering his moto '*If you can grow 'em' I can pick 'em'*. The trees were tall and you had to use tall ladders to reach the fruit.

Because OlaB was limber and light weight, she was chosen to be the one to pick the fruit in the top of the trees. She attached a bucket by a belt around her waist and got ready to climb.

"OlaB, you need to be very careful not to knock off a lot of the leaves or break the small limbs," Zolie cautioned her. "The new growth is where next year's crop will grow."

"I'll be very careful Pop," OlaB replied.

Once the morning warmed up, the hornets and yellow jackets became active. OlaB was not expecting yellow jackets to be buzzing around her head. She began swatting at them, losing her balance, tumbling down, bucket and all, while also knocking down loads of leaves. She remembered that Zolie had said that he didn't want to see many leaves on the ground, so OlaB dug a hole and buried them. OlaB's leaf burial must not have been noticed because the Senator asked Zolie to return the next spring and have his family pick all of his fruit crops, not just the cherries.

Albert and Delia tried to persuade the Edwards to stay in a small house which they owned, located across the road from their house. Zolie considered the idea. Olie and OlaB could go to school. It would be nice to be able to settle down but how could Zolie support the family. That was the question? Zolie knew that OlaB dreamed of staying in one place and he was sure that Olie did also, although Olie never voiced his desire.

Chapter Twenty Three

Zolie decided that he and his family would try finding farm work on the farms near the house where Rose's sister lived. Her sister and her husband owned the little house across the road and Albert and Delia offered to let the Edwards rent it. Zolie then began seriously looking for work.

Olie and OlaB started school there in the fall. It was a strange feeling for the two of them. They both were hopeful that they would be able to go to school like other kids. OlaB found that school was a lot harder than she remembered. Very likely, because she advanced herself two grades! The teachers thought that she was a little behind since she came from another state, so they gave her extra assistance, hoping to bring her up to grade level. The teachers had no idea that OlaB had destroyed her report cards but with their help and the help of her cousins she finally was able to achieve grade level and pass all of her tests. Olie did not seem to have trouble with his studies, but, of course, he had not advanced himself two grade levels.

Zolie had heard from other farm workers who lived nearby, that a man could make good money working in the potato sheds in Idaho. So, he headed to Idaho, leaving Rosa and his children, and spent the winter working in the potato sheds. This was the first time that he had worked away from the family and it felt so strange and wrong that he decided that when the potato sheds closed down for the season he 'would not' work away from the family again.

OlaB enjoyed being with her cousins and being able to have lots of family around. They were constantly playing tricks on one another. One weekend shortly after school started, Albert and Delia decided to visit Albert's brother and spend the night with him. Rosa lived just across the street so they felt safe with leaving their children under her watchful eye and going away overnight.

Delia grew a large variety of flowers in her garden. While she was out picking a huge bouquet to take with them on their trip, OlaB and her cousin, Levon, were in back of OlaB's house painting a big sign to put on the back of Albert's car just before they were to leave. The sign read 'Just Married'.

When Albert and Delia returned home they told about how friendly everyone had been.

"As we would pass, people would wave and shout, 'congratulations and happy honeymoon'," Delia said, hardly able to keep back a smile. "Albert decided that something must be wrong with the car, so he got out and looked it over. That's when he discovered the sign. Since I had this big bouquet in my lap, we must have looked the part."

When Zolie returned from Idaho it was too early in the season for fruit to be ready to pick. He and Albert filled the long hours by studying the Bible. They didn't agree on much, but discussed their different beliefs openly. Albert believed that there was a later day revelation needed to supplement the Bible. Zolie did not share this belief and was determined to learn the scriptures more and more and teach what he studied to Rosa, Olie and OlaB.

In the spring shortly before school was out for the summer, OlaB woke up with a lump under here ear. It didn't hurt so she didn't say anything about it. Zolie had found a job near Provo, Utah, and they were waiting for school to be over before moving. While waiting, OlaB's lump grew larger and by the time they started for Provo, OlaB had developed a fever. While driving through Provo early on the morning they left,

Zolie stopped at the dentist's house. He was the dentist that OlaB had previously been to with a tooth ache. The dentist recommended that OlaB see a doctor instead of him. The doctor recommended applying cool packs. So, they continued on to Zolie's new job.

Zolie parked the truck at the back of the new boss's house. It was late when Zolie and his family arrived and got camp set up. The prior arrangements were that Rosa would use the basement of the bosses' house in which to cook and eat. OlaB was feeling worse and her fever had gotten higher. Olie decided to set up a camp-cot for himself out by the truck for the night, so he wouldn't disturb OlaB's rest.

Mr. James, the new boss, worked until midnight in a plant that froze fruit. When he got home he parked his pickup between Zolie's camp and his house. A little after midnight Zolie got up to give OlaB some aspirins with a drink of water. Just before lying back down, something caught his attention in the corner of his eye. Looking out at Mr. James' truck, Zolie saw a fire burning in the cab. He jumped up, not bothering to dress, and ran to the James' house and began to knock and yell 'fire'.

Mr. James had just gotten to sleep and it took a moment for him to respond to the knocking and yelling. He came running out of his house to see what all of the yelling was about and noticed his truck was on fire. He tried to get into the truck and move it but his truck was too hot to get into. Then he, Zolie and Olie attempted to push the truck away from the house while Mrs. James was calling the fire department.

Two men, who were passing by in a car, stopped, and with their help, the truck was pushed away from the house by the time the fire department got there. The firemen had the fire out in minutes. Mrs. James took Rosa and OlaB into her house while the fire was being extinguished. Mr. James and Zolie realized that they were both still in their underwear so... they both hurriedly got into their pants before entering the house where the ladies were.

"I want to thank you, young lady," Mr. James said to OlaB when he entered the house. "I am certainly glad you were awake."

"I couldn't sleep because of my jaw," OlaB said, holding a cool cloth on her jaw.

"You know, that if we hadn't gotten to the truck as soon as we did, the gas tank might have exploded and we all could have been badly burned or even killed," Mr. James continued.

"I am glad that I was up looking in on OlaB," Zolie said, noticing her swollen jaw. "Things could have been much worse."

"You can call me Robert," Mr. James said. "And, my wife's name is Rachel. I am going to take off work tomorrow to see if we can find a doctor for your daughter."

After going to several different doctors, they found a specialist that decided that the problem was due to an abscessed tooth, so he extracted it. The specialist said that he would have to lance OlaB's jaw and insert a tube to let it drain. After three grueling days of hot salt packs on her jaw, the infection was gone and OlaB was almost back to normal.

Rachel looked in on OlaB over the next few days as she continued to convalesce and while Rosa, Zolie and Olie went to work picking the strawberries. The Edwards and James families had become good friends during the strawberry harvest but soon the job was finished and it was again time to say 'goodbye'. OlaB especially had a hard time saying her goodbyes.

"*It is time to say goodbye again*," OlaB thought. "*This is like saying goodbye to kinfolks. I will never see Mrs. Rachel again. In spite of our different beliefs in God, I remember Rachel saying that she believed God had sent me to save their lives. I believe they saved mine also.*"

Then tears formed in her eyes.

Chapter Twenty Four

It was almost time for the berries to be ready for picking on the Senator's farm, so Zolie headed for the farm. By the time they got there, the dewberries were ready to be picked. The Senator provided heavy leather gloves to help protect their hands from the thorns. This was the first time Zolie and his family had picked dewberries. That was defiantly not their favorite job. But, soon the dewberries were picked and the cherries were ready for picking. The Senator told Zolie that he could pick and can all the cherries that they wanted.

The cherry crop was about finished for the season and when they had completed the picking of the last cherry tree, Zolie decided to move to a camp outside of Layton, Utah, expecting to be able to find farm work near the camp. When the Edwards got to the Layton camp, ten to twelve families had already arrived. All the men were gathered in the center of the camp talking about some orders which had been handed down from the Mormon Church. Zolie had not yet heard about these orders since they had been isolated on the Senator's farm for the last few weeks.

The farmers were ordered not to hire anyone that was not a Mormon, which included everyone in the camp. Consequently, the farmers had to let their vegetable crops rot in the fields rather that hire non-Mormon farm workers. Zolie had saved some money and it was safely put away in 'Rosa's bank', but many of the other families were rapidly running out of cash.

The camp was located on two irrigation canals which carried winter-snow-runoff to water the valley crops, because it didn't rain nearly enough on the valley floor during the growing season. One of the canals was deep and swift but the other one was wide and slow moving and shallow enough to wade in to do the laundry.

It was not uncommon to have mountain rains during the summer. These rains were normally in the mountains above the dam that held the irrigation water. The mountain rains would often cause mud slides. A few nights after the Edwards had arrived in camp, the entire camp was awakened to an enormous display of lighting and thunder. The storm seemed to be in the foothills and everyone knew that a flash-flood, and consequently a mud-slide, could happen at any minute because everyone in camp had seen or lived through such disasters.

The camp was located outside of Layton, Utah, and only one highway ran through the state. Salt Lake City was only twenty-five miles away but a mud-slide could isolate the camp from the outside world. One afternoon at 3:00 o'clock there was a long continuous blast on the town siren. Everyone was accustomed to the siren sounding at 6:00 am, 12:00 noon and 6:00 pm and two long blasts if there were a fire. After a short pause, the siren sounded with a second long blast. Several men of the camp, including Zolie, ran into town and gathered at the City Hall.

"What's going on?" Zollie asked one of the men who was standing on the City Hall steps.

"There has been a massive mud slide up in the mountains," he announced, while tacking an announcement on a bulletin board outside the City Hall. "It has filled the big canal full of mud and boulders the size of a car. In a short time the entire valley will be without water. We are calling for every abled bodied man and boy to grab a shovel and start working to clear the canal as much as possible until the heavy machinery can arrive and get up the mountain."

Each crew worked a twelve-hour shift. Zolie and Olie joined one of the crews, it didn't seem to matter now if you were a Mormon or not!

Water from the two irrigation ditches that ran through camp began to over-flow as the mud forced the water downstream. A young couple had put their tent near the ditch and water was about to wash it away. Some of the men wondered what they should do since no one had seen the couple during the last a few days, so they moved the couples' tent up to dryer ground. That night when the young couple returned, they found all of their belongings moved. The young man went to where the men had gathered around a campfire and thanked them for moving their camp.

"My wife was having a miscarriage and I was afraid to leave her alone," the young man explained. "I had to take her to the hospital and we have been there for the past two days."

After that he became 'one of the boys'.

While the men from the camp were working to clear the mud, the cannery was left without a crew. The cannery owners came to the camp in search of workers to process the supply of green beans that were ready to be canned, so Rosa and OlaB hired on.

When the beans were all canned, and the men were still working on the mud slide, Rosa and OlaB looked for a ride into Salt Lake City to shop for some new clothes. A jockey, who was staying at the camp, said that he was going into town and that Rosa and OlaB could ride with him. They were lucky to get into town in one peace. The jockey drove his car like he rode his horse and the fast ride into town was quite an experience. After Rosa and OlaB finished their shopping they went to the prearranged pick up location but the jockey was nowhere to be seen. They waited and waited and it was getting dark and the jockey finally showed up at 7:30 pm—drunk. If the ride into town was fast, it was nothing compared to the ride home….

The heavy machinery finally arrived at the site of the mud slide and Zolie and Olie headed for the camp. Zolie expected that the ban on workers would be lifted. It had not been and he was more than a little perturbed about the situation, so he called a family meeting.

"I am fearful that we will not be able to work in Utah any longer," he said. "I hear that there is land in Oregon just waiting for someone to farm it."

"Do you mean that we could settle down?" OlaB asked.

"I hear that Oregon in offering the land for settlement," Zolie answered. "I have wanted to see Oregon for some time. This might be the time for us. The jockey, Rodney, and his daughter would like to go with us as far as Idaho."

"I hope that he doesn't drink," Rosa said, and relayed the account to Zolie about their trip into Salt Lake City.

"They will be driving their own car," Zolie said, asking Rosa more about their shopping trip.

The Edwards prepared for the trip by taking along several cans of food and a ten-gallon-can of water. The trip from Utah to Oregon covered a lot of desert. They had gone about 100 miles into the desert when they discovered that they had only one gallon of water left. Olie had failed to check the can before they left on the trip.

There was nothing but hot dry desert before them. The road was gravel, sand and very rough. About half way across the desert, the wiring on the truck got too hot and caught on fire. Zolie was able to get the fire put out but the engine would not restart. It was now getting late and Rodney didn't have time to get into town and buy the wiring needed to repair the truck before the stores closed. They set up camp beside the road and rationed their water.

Times were hard and people were getting desperate, robberies along a highway were not uncommon. Luckily, that night there were not many people on the road. They ate from the canned food and took only a few swallows of water. Zolie, Olie and Rodney took turns standing watch that night. Some wolves tried coming into camp but Rodney's large German shepherd kept them away.

"We need to get a dog," Olie said the next morning, thinking about the wolves. "A good dog could help watch the camp and help warn us if someone or something got too close."

"I'll see what I can find," Zolie replied.

A few cars passed by during the night, throwing rocks as they passed. By morning, a lantern which Zolie had lit and put behind the truck was so battered that it had to be thrown away. Zolie and Rodney went into the nearest town and bought the wiring to repair the truck. After the truck was repaired and they were back on the road it was getting late in the afternoon as they approached a town beside a river. OlaB and Rosa were so happy to see a town again. Everything was fresh and green.

A few days later Rodney and his daughter left the Edwards and headed north while the Edwards headed farther west. There was nothing but barren desert as far as one could see. As they started going up into some hills they heard a loud bang and the truck rolled to a stop. Zolie and Olie got out to investigate and discovered that they had broken a back axle. Luckily, they were in front of a country store and garage. The owner didn't have an axle to repair the truck but he went several miles into the closest town and returned with the needed parts.

Several hot and dry days later, they crossed into Oregon, but the scenery didn't change. It was still desert with only a scrubby tree here and there. At a little past noon, they were all tired and hungry.

"I'm hungry," Zolie said, frustrated with the desert and the heat. "I think that I remember a 'tree' a few miles back."

With that, Zolie turned around and headed for the tree. It was a little more than a bush but he stopped and they ate lunch and he never turned back around!

"What a disappointment," Zolie remarked. "Why would anyone want to come here? There's supposed to be good farming in the Klamath Valley but all I can see is this dry desert land, not even a tree can grow here."

After turning around to go back to the small shade to eat their lunch, Zolie didn't turn around again but headed east. He figured that they could make it to Louisiana for the strawberry harvest by the next spring. They would have time to stop by Rosa's sister's home in Utah for a night or two on the way, and possibly stop by Kansas to see their friend, John Thomas in Pittsburg.

"It was good to see our old friend, John again," Zolie said, after saying a final goodbye and heading for Louisiana.

"I'll miss John too," Rosa said and Olie and OlaB echoed their feelings.

It was late December when the Edwards rolled into the small, dreary coal mining town of Henryetta, Oklahoma. Zolie went in search of a job in the coal industry until the Louisiana strawberries would be ripe and ready to pick. There were no coal mining jobs to be found. Work was getting harder and harder to find and wages were almost nothing.

Zolie called his family together. "We must have a family meeting. You kids know how hard times are and you both are growing up. Do we need to settle down in one place so you two can meet friends your ages? Should we get a farm and settle down and live off the farm, or should we keep going on down the road like we have been doing?"

It was Christmas Eve and OlaB and Olie voted to settle down on a farm and raise what they needed. The blue day turned into a bright shinny day and after the traditional Christmas dinner everyone slept well that night.

Chapter Twenty Five

Life in the Ozarks—

Zolie headed east out of Henryetta, Oklahoma, toward Arkansas. He reminisced about those past years when the family first began working as farm laborers when they went to Louisiana to pick strawberries. As they left Oklahoma and entered into Arkansas, life seemed to be coming full-circle. They had been good years but Zolie and his family were ready to settle down, so he continued on toward the research farm where his farm work began. Zolie stopped in each town which they passed through, inquiring about farmland for sale.

It was getting late when they entered Prairie Grove, Arkansas. The family rented a cabin for the night and Zolie made plans to go to the local feed store the first thing the next morning, expecting that this would be the location where the local farmers would gather to discuss the daily news and buy the feed that would be needed for their cattle. Zolie was correct, several farmers were gathered there when he arrived. He began asking around if anyone knew of a farm for sale.

Soon a gentleman came over to where Zolie was standing.

"Howdy, my name is Edd Percifield, and I have a farm for sale," Edd said, introducing himself.

In discussing the sales transaction, Zolie learned that Edd was being forced to sell his farm or the bank was going to foreclose. This didn't concern Zolie as long as he was able to get a clear title.

"I'm sorry to hear about the reason that you are having to sell your farm," Zolie quietly mentioned to Edd.

"It is just one of the hazards of our time," Edd slowly replied, feeling that there was no other way out for him and his family.

"Let's go see the place," Zolie said. "I have a truck loaded with all our belongings, hop in and let's go have a look, you can show me the way."

"We can go as far as the turnoff, but from there I'll pick up my wagon," Edd explained. "Your truck can't make it to the farm over the last mile or so. It is just a wagon lane."

Zolie went by the cabin to tell Rosa about the farm place which he was going to look over. Then he picked up Edd and they travelled in the truck as far as the turn off where Edd had left his team and wagon. The farm was located back in the hills fifteen miles from Prairie Grove. Off the main road, the wagon trail led to the farm. The trail was cut through the timber, exposing a rocky base resembling a creek bed, but somewhat rougher.

It was in early January and Zolie looked over a portion of the farm and checked the soil. He was thankful that some of the land appeared to have been cleared. After looking over the farm, Zolie got back into Edd's wagon and went to where he had parked the truck.

"I will have to sell my truck as part of the down payment," Zolie said. "I hope that won't be a problem with you."

"I don't believe that will be a problem," Edd replied. "When will you want to move in? My family and I have no place to move into. I hadn't expected to sell so soon and I haven't even made any arrangements to move."

"You and your family can live with us until you find a place," Zolie said. "Just tell me how I am going to get our belongings up to the farm, you said my truck can't make it over the wagon trail, and after seeing it, I surely believe you!"

On the day Zolie and his family planned to move in, Edd and his family had previously made plans to go to Edd's sister's farm for the day and butcher their hogs for their winter's meat.

"I'll tie the team and wagon to the same tree we used the other day, Edd said. "You can park the truck there and load your belongings onto the wagon."

The road from Prairie Grove to the turnoff was not much better than the wagon trail. But Zolie found Edd's wagon tied to the tree where he told him it would be, so Zolie and Olie loaded everything onto the wagon and started down the hill to the farm. After traveling about a mile, they came to a house and saw a man chopping wood out by his wood pile. OlaB noticed some women in the house, peeping out from behind the curtains.

"They don't look very friendly," OlaB whispered, trying not to stare. "Mom, do you think that they know that we are moving in?"

"Are we close to the Percifield place?" Zolie asked the man, trying to be neighborly.

"Yep…, just a half mile on down the road," he slowly replied, after waiting a long time before answering.

Zolie just sat there for a while, wondering whether and how they were going to fit in at this new place, waiting patiently for the man to say something else.

Finally, Olie said, "Pop, I think that you are going to have to step on the gas or are we going to sit here all day."

Zolie laughed at what Olie had said and popped the reins and the horses started moving. He had seen the neighbor's house when he and Edd looked at the new farm. He had not told Rosa about having near-by neighbors and he had not mentioned anything about their new farm house yet. Soon they came to a hill and when they reached the top, what a beautiful picture lay before them. Down the hill was a cedar-tree-lined, sandy lane and at the end of the lane stood a house and barn along with several out buildings. The house had a white picket fence around it and Rosa could just imagine the yard filled with blooming flowers.

"Oh, what a beautiful place," Rosa said, amazed at the sight. "Oh, Zolie, is this going to be our new home!"

Moving into a house of strangers, without them even being there yet, was different and a little interesting. Rosa and OlaB looked over the house while Zolie and Olie began unloading the wagon. The house was thankfully very clean and neat but was sparsely furnished. At the end of the front room, stood a working fireplace made of native rock and equipped with a handle to hold a pot, so Rosa would be able to cook a pot of beans over the wood fire. Zolie could already taste them, and he started dreaming of Rosa's famous corn bread as well.

"What is that strange sound?" OlaB questioned, turning to Rosa. "Do you hear it? There it is again."

Rosa and OlaB looked around for the source of the strange sound. They looked in corners, behind furniture, and much to their surprise, they found two doves in a box under a bed. They surmised that the doves must be pets! Living in the hills was going to be a whole new experience!

OlaB looked out the windows and all she could see was trees. She had been afraid of the woods since childhood after hearing her mom tell stories about all kinds of animals that lived in the Arkansas hills. Olie, on the other hand was delighted with all the trees. He could imagine all sorts of adventures and times to come that he could going hunting in them.

"Pop," Olie questioned. "When can I go hunting and exploring in all these woods? I just can't wait."

It was getting dusky dark and the Edwards heard the sound of a wagon coming up the lane, knowing that it had to be the Percifield family. Rosa was very anxious to meet them, but at the same time, she was a little nervous. After all, they were going to be living in and sharing the Percifield's old house. In her mind she thought, 'what has Zolie gotten us into now!'

The meeting of the two families was congenial, and after a while, the feeling was like meeting kinfolks returning from a long absence. Kizzie Percifield and Rosa soon felt as though they were related to each other like sisters. In no time Thelma and OlaB acted as though they had known each other their entire lives.

During the two weeks before the Percifield family found a place of their own, the two families cooked and visited with each other daily. Kizzie loved hearing about the things on the 'outside'. Kizzie seldom left the hills to go into town, which was the situation for most of the women living in the hills.

While the women were visiting and getting acquainted, Edd took Zolie and Olie around to some of the other farms and into Prairie Grove looking for a good team for Zolie. Along with the team of horses, Zolie also bought a sow that was expecting pigs and a cow that had just had a heifer calf. He also bought several laying hens and two roosters. Their farm was growing.

Zolie and Olie went into town with the new team and one of the Percifield's wagons and came home with four chairs for the living room, three bedsteads and lumber to make a dining table and a cook table for the kitchen. After a while the Edwards' house was furnished just as well as everyone else's house. After the Percifields found a house of their own and moved in, the two families were still fast friends and were together at least two nights a week.

Much to Zolie's and Rosa's surprise, Thelma Percifield had previously arranged to have a party at her house before it became the Edwards' house. Thelma asked Zolie what she should do. Zolie told her that she should not cancel the party, that it would be a good way for Olie and OlaB to be able to meet the young people from the hills.

Since the Percifield family had accepted the Edwards family, the other hill people had also accepted them. Generally speaking, hill people didn't accept outsiders, possibly because of the illegal stills set up in the woods, not knowing whom they could really trust.

There was a large crowd at the party. Thelma had already told OlaB about life in the hills. There were over eighteen girls of dating age and thirty boys. Mountain girls were taught at an early age how to make and care for a garden, cook, and keep a house clean and in order. A lot of the girls were married by the age of sixteen and OlaB doubted that they had ever been out of the hills.

The house was very large and it along with the yard were full of young people. Olie and OlaB dressed in their best clothes but OlaB's dress was way too young looking for her, so Kizzie told Rosa that she would make OlaB some new dresses. Kizzie could look at a picture of a dress and cut out her own pattern and make a dress that looked just like the picture. Rosa had a lot of material packed away in one of the clothes trunks so she gave some of it to Kizzie to make OlaB a new dress.

The party went well, they played games, sang songs and visited with one another till almost midnight. OlaB was smitten by the young man that led the singing. He was about five feet eleven inches tall with a beautiful voice. He had black, wavy hair and clear blue eyes and his name was Lawrence Sawyer. He was twenty-three years old and not married but his age didn't bother OlaB. Most of the boys over twenty were already married.

Moving to the hills was like taking a giant step back in time. There were no cars so a riding horse or wagon was the only mode of transportation. Families would meet at the school house for singings and church services on weekends and Wednesday nights. Almost everyone went to these events. There were no radios so those weekly get-to-gathers were the only means of learning what was happening on the outside. There were only a few weekly newspapers and when the owner would finish reading his paper he would pass it around to his neighbors.

OlaB had always wanted to have a book around as her friend. Olie liked to read also but it was not an obsession with him as it was with OlaB. She and Olie continued their Bible study with Zolie and Rosa that they had started back in Nebraska. Growing up with a book in her hand, gave OlaB an idealistic view of the world, so she lived most of her life with her head in the clouds, not seeing the real world. An elderly man that lived near the school house put in a library that OlaB visited frequently after school. If a neighbor had a book of any kind, they would donate it to the library.

There were various religious denominations within five miles of their farm but everyone met in the school house on Sundays. After attending the church service, OlaB and Olie would discuss what the preacher had said and compare it to what they read in the Bible. They concluded that none of the preachers taught exactly like what they had read. So their major Bible education would still continue at home. Surely, somewhere there must be a group of people that believed the Bible like OlaB and Olie did, this was their dream.

On Sunday afternoons, after church, groups of young people would gather at one of their houses for dinner and afterward they would go down to one of the mountain streams and wade in the water, or if the water was deep enough, they would go canoeing. There were a lot of streams and caves to explore. On week-ends, life was full of adventures for the young people because most farm chores were done early in the mornings.

Shortly after Zolie and his family got settled into their farm house, and the farm was up and running, he and Olie went to work on the wagon trail from the road up to the house. The neighbors must have thought that they were crazy but they wanted to be able to get a truck up to the house. Zolie missed his truck, which he had to sell, but he planned to soon get another one. He and Olie spent a lot of time working on the road between doing their farm work.

It would take them almost two years to complete the road and make it passable for a car. Zolie went to the county commissioner and convinced the county that the road from Prairie Grove should be drivable. Zolie planned to buy his small truck as soon as he could.

After a long winter of conditioning themselves to hill life, spring arrived and it was time to go to work. Zolie and Rosa made a big garden and he and Olie planted field corn, cotton, head feed, peanuts and popcorn. The farm had an established orchard of peaches and apples. They had a good crop of vegetables but the cotton crop was poor. After the seeds were picked out, there was only enough cotton to card and make batting for quilts.

OlaB cut sprouts growing from the tree roots using a 'grubbing hoe'. The tree roots had not previously been removed on the cleared land. Olie and Zolie were kept busy plowing the crops to keep the weeds down.

There was an abundance of wild strawberries, blackberries, blueberries and wild plums in the woods as well as chinquapins, walnuts and hickory nuts. Once the forest bounty was gathered and the fresh vegetables gathered, Zolie loaded everything on the wagon and headed for town in hopes of selling them.

Times were getting harder and no one had money to buy much. The store owners in Fayetteville, Arkansas, would exchange Zolie's produce for such things as flour, sugar, baking powder and cocoa. After canning and drying all that they could, the Edwards family had plenty of food on the table but no money.

When school opened the next fall, Olie and OlaB again started to school. Olie only got to go a short time to the ninth grade before having to drop out to help Zolie on the farm. The schools which they had attended in Utah were scholastically ahead of the Arkansas schools, so OlaB was able to breeze through the seventh-grade and the eighth grade was also easy. When OlaB had time on her hands she kept occupied writing poetry.

Many of the school kids had never seen a train, a swimming pool, gone shopping, worked for money or seen a hundred acres of cotton or corn in one field. The kids at school were interested in hearing about the outside and OlaB was constantly kept busy telling about places she had been and things she had done.

The hill people took care of their own. When a woman got sick or it was her time to give birth, a few of the neighbor women would come into her home and take care of her for a week to a week and a half until she was strong enough to carry on with her cooking and housework. When a man became sick and unable to work, some of the neighbor men would take care of him and take care of the farm shores until he was again able.

There were several midwives in the hills and two of them would come and help the woman in giving childbirth. Most all of the babies in the hills were delivered at home, but a few women decided to go to the clinic in Prairie Grove. There was an old man that had read several medical books and had learned, from his parents and grandparents, how to use native herbs. His reputation was known all over the hills and many families called on him to tend to their sick.

When a person died, some of their close neighbors would come and wash and dress the body and lay the body out on a door until the coffin was completed. Since there was no way to embalm the body, this was the best they could do. An older couple that lived down the road from the Edwards kept walnut lumber in their attic to dry out and be used to make coffins. After a death, the men would gather together and make the coffin.

Also, when a person in the hills died, the women would take food for a meal after the funeral and someone from each family was expected to attend the funeral. OlaB was elected by the Edwards family to represent them. She also helped with the singing at funerals.

Zolie had grown sorghum and during the winter months he and Olie rigged up a crushing wheel to extract the juice from the cane. They then constructed a long metal vat and cooked the juice, stirring constantly until it became syrupy. Rosa and OlaB learned how to cook with the molasses and made the most delicious peanut candy and popcorn balls. These became very popular items for their weekly parties.

That winter, Zolie taught Olie how to butcher their hogs. From the rendered fat they made lard and soap and from the jowls they made mincemeat. Zolie penned up the hogs that he planned to butcher for several weeks before butchering and fed them all the corn they could eat. This made the meat taste much better and the other farmers also began feeding their hogs corn before butchering.

When the neighbors found out that Zolie could tell if a hen was laying or sitting they kept him busy culling their flocks. His expertise with farming and farm animals was known throughout the hill country.

Kizzie had taught OlaB how to sew and Zolie had found an old Singer sewing machine. Unfortunately, the machine was completely disassembled. Zolie was able to reassemble the parts and only had to buy a shuttle. Then the machine sewed like a dream. OlaB now was able to use the material from the feed sacks to make underwear, sheets, curtains and tea towels.

The Edwards family were set for the winter. Several sacks of dried beans and peas were treated to prevent weevils and stored in one of the out buildings. Another out building served as a smoke house. Zolie followed the instructions of the hill farmers and he quickly learned how to bury potatoes, turnips, sweet potatoes and cabbages in the ground and cover them with straw and soil. Neighbors taught each other the skills that they had learned and their information was shared willingly.

Life was good and there was plenty of food, but, there was one big problem! There was no money to buy new shoes and new clothes from the mail-order catalogs. Hopefully the next year after selling the crops and settling up with all the creditors, there would be a little left for a new pair of shoes for everyone.

Chapter Twenty Six

On the Road Again

In the early fall, Zolie called a family meeting.

"I know that we voted to buy a farm and settle down, and we have," Zolie began. "But, our work clothes will not make it through another season."

Olie asked, "Why don't we go to Texas again and pick cotton?"

"That was also what I was thinking," Zolie answered.

"That should give us enough money to buy some new work clothes," Rosa said. "I don't think I can put another patch on our old clothes.

"I was hoping that we could find another way," OlaB chimed in disappointedly. "We said we were tired of moving around."

"I won't sell the farm," Zolie commented. "We will come back after the cotton season is over."

"I just hate to have to leave all our friends, even for just a little while," OlaB said sadly.

By the end of August the Edwards loaded up the new truck which Zolie had recently bought. He had to sale his big truck as a part of the payment on the farm. They now headed for west Texas and the cotton fields. The new truck was small but they would make it work. The farmer in Texas that they had previously contracted with had a house in which they could live.

OlaB hated to move away from her new 'boyfriend' but she needed new clothes and told him she would be back in three months. Olie didn't have a girlfriend though he had dated a few girls. To him the move to Texas seemed more like an adventure and the girls would still be there when he returned.

The family worked hard on Mr. Purnell's farm. The Purnell farm had 125 acers of the best cotton the Edwards had ever seen. Along with the small house, they had all the milk and eggs they wanted and also were able to help themselves to the large vegetable garden. Rosa made all the butter which they could eat.

The house had only two rooms, but Mr. Purnell had two extra bedrooms in the farm house and told Zolie that his kids could have them for sleeping since they were such good workers.

Each morning, Zolie and Olie would be sitting on the row waiting for it to get light enough to start picking and Rosa and OlaB would go to the field as soon as they got dinner cooked. So that they wouldn't lose time, Rosa and OlaB brought the food to the field and found a shady place to keep it until noon. The meal generally consisted of a pot of beans and a pot of potatoes, cornbread, fried meat and something sweet. Zolie and his family had hired out as a crew that could pick a bale of cotton a day. Zolie and Olie would have to pick 600 pounds each and Rosa and OlaB 400 pounds each.

Picking cotton was heavy work. After picking 75 to 80 pounds of cotton, the sack became very heavy to drag on the ground behind you. This would also cause holes to be worn into the sack, making it unusable.

"Pop, you'll have to come and help me carry my sack, it's just too heavy and I can't budge it, I'll bet the thing weighs 100 pounds," OlaB complained.

Zolie answered her, "O.K. Sis, I'll dump your sack but you'll have to pick in mine while I'm gone, we can't waste a bit of down-time, time's money, you know."

Olie was the one who would run to his Mom so he could empty her cotton sack and then she would continue picking in his.

Mr. Purnell weighed in Zolie and his family the first day and after that, they were allowed to do their own weighing. When Zolie said it was a bale, Mr. Purell would take it to the gin and it would always weigh 10 to 20 pounds over. Mr. Purell paid Zolie for the work that the family did, and Rosa kept if in her 'bank'. The first two weeks Zolie let Olie and OlaB keep all they could earn to buy clothes. Back then, a nice coat cost ten dollars, and shoes between two and three dollars.

*****

The cotton picking season was over and Olie and OlaB were glad to once again be back in the Arkansas hills and back to their friends. While working in Texas, there was no time to get acquainted with anyone, so dating had to be put on the back burner.

The hill people had their own code of conduct that was to be followed between a boy and girl when they were dating. A hill girl did not ride horseback with her boyfriend. A dating couple could hold hands or walk arm in arm with each other. But, they never kissed goodnight until after several dates and then never in public. If a girl got pregnant before she was married, she and the baby, along with her parents, would become outcasts unless there was a shot-gun wedding.

OlaB was thankful that her friend, Thelma, had taught her and Olie the ways of the hills so that they would never do anything or act anyway inappropriately. The hill kids thought that OlaB, and sometimes Olie, were funny because they addressed older people as Mr. or Mrs. They would answer with Sir or Ma'am and with a 'thank you' for things people did for them. They said please a lot and never said ain't. They had been taught well in the schools while in Utah.

127

Zolie had told OlaB that she was too young to have a boyfriend so when she and Olie would leave a party and start walking home, Olie would walk ahead of OlaB and her boyfriend and before they neared their house she and Olie would walk on home alone. If Olie had a date then OlaB and her boyfriend would sit on a rock and wait until Olie arrived and she and Olie would then go home together. This worked fine until Zolie caught on to their shenanigans.

The kids in the hills knew Zolie wouldn't allow OlaB to date. They knew that Olie dated and wondered why OlaB could not. Soon all the kids knew she wanted to date so they decided on a scheme to help her out. They would keep a watch out for Zolie and let OlaB know, if she were with a boy, that her Pop was coming. The boy OlaB was with would let go of her arm and a girl would take his place. The few times that Zolie showed up, he never let on that he knew their game, but it served his purpose of being a watchful dad.

When a girl was allowed to start dating, she would invite her date to her home. They always had to stay in the kitchen because most of the parents had their beds in the living room. The girls made sure that their home was clean and everything was in its place. If she was really interested in the boy, she would always have something good cooked to serve to him so he would know she was a good cook and a good housekeeper.

In the spring and fall it was not uncommon for someone to get careless and leave a fire unattended in the fireplace or on the stove. All the people would band together and fight the fire. If a fire caused a family to lose their home then the men in the community would come with their saws, hammers, levels and any other tools that they had and rebuild a four-room house for them. The hills were mostly covered in timber so lumber was not a problem.

Once the house was finished, some of the men would take wagons and go for miles around collecting house-keeping items. Everyone was always very generous. Some would give bowls or snuff-glasses, homemade quilts and feather pillows. Things didn't match but they didn't have to. Cups and saucers and small bowls came in boxes of oats, and a family would eat oats until they collected or traded enough to make a set of six or eight.

Life in the hills was very modest, people learned to use and make-do with whatever was available. For example, a typical breakfast in the hills consisted of biscuits and gravy with scrambled eggs and side-meat (bacon). There was always plenty of jelly or honey. They also ate a lot of oatmeal, if the family was collecting cups and saucers. There was always coffee and milk to drink.

There was always fried or boiled potatoes and fried pork at dinner, the noon meal. Rosa often hung an iron pot in the fire place and slow cooked beans or soup all morning. She would cook green beans with side meat when fresh beans were in season. In the spring, young shoots of poke greens would be gathered, parboiled, and cooked with side meat. The meal was always served with cornbread and a custard pie or fruit pie, in season, or bread pudding made from the left-over morning biscuits. Rosa delighted in making loves of fresh bread, and anyone that had ever eaten her loaves of bread knew she was the best baker ever! When company would come home on Sundays the family was treated with chicken and dumplings or chicken and dressing and a cake which was baked the day before.

In the hills, by the age of thirteen, girls knew how to cook, sew and keep house. They had been taught by their moms since the age of six or seven. At an early age they would start making a 'hope chest' and they were expected to have it full of quilts, towels and sheets and pillow cases by the time they got married. As soon as a boy was old enough, he would help his dad take care of the pigs and chickens and milk the cows. He learned how to plow and tend to the crops. As soon as he knew enough to provide for a family, he was ready for marriage.

Weddings were not a big affair. When a couple wanted to get married, they just simply slipped over to the preacher's home and quietly got married. When the other young people found out that the couple had gotten married it was everything but quiet. Everyone would gather at the couple's house, the night of their wedding day, and give them a charivari (called a shivaree by the hill folks) and a 'pounding'. It would turn into a big noisy party lasting well into the next morning, with guests bringing a pound of some kind of food.

Zolie had learned what kinds of produce and about how much the local merchants would trade for flour, sugar and a few other items that he could not raise so Zolie would not over-plant. Most people did not have money to actually buy farm produce, not even the merchants. Zolie and Olie made a few trips into Fayetteville in an attempt to sale their farm produce, but few there had enough money to buy anything either.

On one of Zolie's trips into town, he met a man and his wife that were trying to barter for some food.

"I have some green beans and potatoes that I can give you," Zolie said approaching the gentleman and offering him his hand. "My name is Zolie Edwards, and I have a farm a few miles outside of town."

"That would be very kind of you," Will Gasbar said turning to his wife. "This is my wife, Faye. We are new in town and are in the process of buying a few acers in the area."

They continued talking and Zolie learned that the acreage Will was buying was located next to the Edwards' farm. Will had been hurt seriously in the war and was now receiving a small government pension. The pension was not enough for them to live on the outside, so they decided to move to the hill country. Zolie and Olie helped the Gasbars build a two-room house and in the spring Zolie taught Will and Faye how to make a garden.

That summer Zolie made a deal with Will Gasbar. He suggested that Will and his wife, Faye, move into their house in the fall and care for their livestock while they picked cotton in Texas. Olie agreed to sleep in the Gasbar's house, which was only a quarter of a mile away, until the Edwards left for Texas. During that fall, while the Edwards were in Texas, Faye could sale or trade the eggs and cream and they could eat whatever they wanted from the Edwards' farm. They were also given a small payment to care for the livestock.

Zolie contacted the Purcell's and made arrangements to again pick the fall cotton on their farm. Olie and Zolie loaded their truck and headed for west Texas again.

Chapter Twenty Seven

Mr. Purnell was very pleased to have the Edwards crew pick his cotton for another year. He had begun looking for pickers, but when he received the letter from Zolie asking about the possibility of his family picking the cotton for him another year, he told Zolie that he would stop looking and that he would only hire others if Zolie thought that his crew could not finish before the cold weather. Mr. Purnell offered Zolie and his family the same arrangements as they had agreed upon the previous year.

Rayford, the Purnell's only son, was about Olie's age and had grown up not having to work. Olie and Rayford would pal around some on the weekends and after work. Rayford usually was the one that went to the mail box and one day he came back with a sample box of Exlax. He wasn't aware of what Exlax was and he was thinking that it was candy, so, he ate all 12 of the squares. He told Olie what he had found. Olie knew about Exlax and told Rayford what Exlax was used for. Olie came to Rosa and told her what Rayford had done. They both had a good laugh at Rayford's expense.

That weekend, after Rayford recovered from his 'candy misadventure', he was invited to a party and asked OlaB to go with him. He was allowed to drive the family car and she accepted his invitation. OlaB soon discovered that the kids in West Texas were a different breed than the kids to which she was accustomed. The kids at the party talked about things, in mixed company, that the hill girls wouldn't talk about even to another girl. She was very glad when Rayford dropped her home.

As usual when the Edwards family started another job, work was hard and long, and they all worked six days a week. Sundays were used for washing the week's dirty clothes. Clothes-washing was done out-of-doors in cast iron wash pots over a wood fire and using a rub board and home-made lye soap. They would wear the same work clothes for at least a couple of days.

Rosa and OlaB made their own cotton-picking sacks out of unbleached burlap. The sacks were 14 feet long with a drawstring at the bottom so that they could more easily empty the cotton which they had just picked. The sacks had a wide strap which went over the shoulder allowing the sack to be pulled behind them.

Mr. Purnell would tease OlaB about her cotton sack having rough hulls in it and he would have to put Rosa's sack on top of hers to sit on as he took the cotton to the gin. Rosa was a skilled cotton picker.

When the Edwards began their cotton picking, Mr. Purnell stayed in the field most of the day, but soon he was offered a job at the gin as the 'ginner'. Zolie was then hired to take the cotton to the gin each day as the cotton picking was completed. He would use Mr. Purnell's team of horses to take the cotton and then ride one of them back to the farm. The round-trip was four miles and Zolie was grateful for the extra pay, which was great for the family.

There was a general store down the road about a half mile and the owners lived in the back of the store. They were good people and sold the food as cheaply as stores in the larger towns of Wheeler and Shamrock, Texas. The Edwards began buying all of their groceries there, except for apples, since they had brought an entire cotton sack full from Arkansas. Rosa made apple pies, and she baked, fried, and made apple butter. They also had all the fresh apples which they wanted to eat. The owners of the general store were Frank and Alma Smith and they actually had a radio!

They would invite the Edwards family each Saturday night to come and join them in listening to 'The Grand Ole Opry', and they insisted that the Edwards family stay until the store closed.

Olie mentioned to the family one Saturday night, as they were leaving, "I really enjoyed listening to the 'Grand Ole Opry' on the radio tonight, do you think we will ever have a radio one of these days?"

OlaB immediately chimed in, "Oh, Pop, Mom, a radio would be so great!"

"I don't think that's possible right now, youngsters," Zolie replied. "Maybe, someday."

One day Mrs. Purnell stepped on a rusty nail and she developed an infection in her foot. Mr. Purnell took her to a doctor and the next day Rosa and OlaB stopped to look in on her on their way to pick cotton. The doctor had told her to soak her foot continually but when they arrived at her house, Mrs. Purnell was delirious with a high fever. They stayed with her and made her more comfortable by bathing her head in cool water. They were still there at noontime when Mr. Purnell had gotten home for lunch.

As Mr. Purnell came into the house, he asked. "What's going on here? You have been here all morning taking care of my wife! I have never met people who are as unselfish and caring as your family."

Rosa answered. "We came by just to check on her and found her delirious and she needed us more than we needed to be working. There is no way we would have left her unattended."

Mr. Purnell answered her, "Mrs. Edwards, we are planning to move to the gin by next year's picking season and if your family comes to pick for us again, I insist that you move into our house while you are working for us."

*****

The Edwards left the Texas Panhandle in late November to go back home to Arkansas. They had made enough in the cotton fields to be able for each to buy a pair of new shoes and a new set of clothes. The trip back home was a long hard trip. The truck had only one seat and it was cold outside so all four of them tried to ride in the cab. Olie sat between Zolie and Rosa and OlaB tried to sit on Rosa's lap. The traveling conditions were certainly uncomfortable but no one complained because everyone was anxious to get back home and besides, sitting jam-packed helped them to keep warm. Finally, Olie decided to bundle up and ride in the back of the truck when it warmed up a little the following day.

As they approached the hill country the odor of wood smoke smelled good to them. In the hills everyone used wood to heat their homes, where-as in Texas, coal was used. They drove straight through, driving from two in the morning until two the next morning.

The hogs were ready to butcher when the Edwards got home. The Gazbars had taken good care of the farm.

"Olie and I are going to start the butchering in the morning," Zolie told Will Gazbar when they had finished looking over the hogs. "We would like for you to help if you feel up to it."

"I know nothing about butchering but I have seen quite enough of dead and mangled humans and animals," Will replied. "Never the less, I would be happy to help in any way that I can."

Edd and Kizzie began a tradition of coming over during butchering time and Zolie and Olie would reciprocate when the Percifields did their butchering. Rosa and Kizzie were involved making and canning sausage while the men cut and cured the meat, getting it ready for the smoke house. After canning the sausage, Rosa began getting things ready to make mincemeat.

"Rosa, I would love to learn how you make your mincemeat, how do you make it so delicious?" Kizzie asked. "Everyone around these parts raves about your mincemeat pies."

"I's a long process, taking the biggest part of two days," Rosa said as she began explaining the method. "Maybe we could get Edd to help us. I have just the job for him."

"First thing I do is to get the hog heads and the scrap meat that the men bring in to me after butchering," Rosa began. Then after cooking the meat for several hours…."

"How do you get the meat off the head?" Kizzie questioned.

Rosa answered. "After the hog's head is boiled and cooled, we can then pull the meat from the jowls. It doesn't take too long it do that way."

Kizzie then asked. "Okay, what comes next? This is sounding like it will take forever."

"Don't you worry your little head any, Kizzie, we will get Edd collared and in here to use the hand grinder to get the meat ground up fairly fine," Rosa answered. "We can have OlaB feed the meat into the grinder and things will go a lot faster."

"When does the fruit and spices get into the mix?" Kizzie asked.

"While Edd and OlaB grind the meat, we will get the fruit cooked and the spices mixed up and mixed with the fruit to set and blend," Rosa answered. "I use canned peaches, dried apples, dried apricots, raisins, prunes oranges and several different spices."

"So, Rosa, you let the mixture set overnight and then mix the meat into this mixture?" Kizzie asked. "The next morning everything will be combined and mixed and then put into quart jars and canned?"

"Yes, this will make between 50 and 60 quarts," Rosa replied. "I make this each winter season, Zolie and Olie especially love mincemeat pies."

Most of the time when the Percifield and Edwards families got together Thelma and OlaB had the job of cooking the meals. Rosa and Kizzie sat and visited and the men did the same. That would make Thelma and OlaB feel like they were being over-worked, so one day as they were making mincemeat pies for the after-dinner desert, OlaB started to take one out of the oven and burned her hand. As she did, she dropped the pie on the floor, then they picked it up and fed it to the adult table that evening, without telling them the reason it was so messy. However, their floors were kept rather clean by scrubbing them with sand and lye water twice a week, so no one got sick, and they were never told about this until the girls were grown.

When OlaB would visit Thelma, they always helped Kizzie in the kitchen, and most of the time OlaB's job was to churn the milk. OlaB hated the boring job of churning, so she would hunt up a book to read as she churned. Kizzie soon learned to tell Thelma to hide their books so OlaB would have to spend her time spinning her tales about the 'life outside'. Kizzie was always hungering for more information about other people and places. Kizzie, as well as most all of the hill women, rarely got the chance to travel anywhere. But, she had a sister who lived in Fort Smith, and for two weeks every summer she would let Thelma visit her sister, wanting Thelma to have the chance she never had, to learn about other areas. Thelma's dad was too heavy to ride with her on houseback, so Zollie volunteered to take her. This was something he did for several summers.

*****

In the early spring, Zolie was beginning to get the 'itchy foot' again.

"Rosa, we're not making any money here in Arkansas, we are making it O.K. but we are just not making any money," Zollie said as he was dreading the idea of asking her and the kids to pull up stakes. "What do you think about going to Louisiana for a few weeks for the strawberry harvest? This will give us a chance to make a little spending money."

"If this is what you think we should do, sure, we'll go," Rosa replied. "You and the kids have been working hard ever since we have been here in Arkansas, maybe this will give us something to think about. It is getting to the point of realizing that living here is not going to better us. The farm cannot produce enough for us to live on."

So, in the spring, Zolie asked Will Gazbar to move back into their home and care for the stock while they went to the Louisiana strawberry fields. They were to tend the garden and keep it hoed but OlaB knew she'd have to cut the big sprouts out of the garden again, because they did not do a good job of that. They could not stay away very long because they would have to get back in time to plant the spring crops.

So, off they went to Louisiana! 'On the road again!'

Chapter Twenty Eight

"I'm working myself to death here in the Arkansas hills," Zolie said, opening up the family meeting. "We've been here for several years now and over the last few years I have worn out three wallets and still don't have two bits to my name! We need to find a place where we can make enough to at least be able to buy a new pair of shoes."

"I've been happy here," OlaB chimed in. "I thought everything was going good. We have a nice house to live in and plenty of food to eat."

"I know," Zolie replied. "But that isn't enough. We can't make enough money here on the farm to buy the things that we need. We are poor and everyone in the hills is also poor. This is partly due to the times we live in, but people on the outside of the hills seem to be better off. The Purnell's seem to be doing O.K."

"Why can't we continue going to West Texas and picking cotton for the Purnell's, Olie asked? "They seem to like us and I'm sure that they would hire us in the fall."

"We could go on picking cotton for the Purnell's," Zolie answered. "But, at the end of the year we still would not have two cents to rub together. I don't think we'll ever have a future here."

"We lived in Arkansas when I married you," Rosa interjected. "We moved to Mississippi looking for something better. Then to Missouri, then to Nebraska and Maryland. Each time looking for something better. We have made a full circle, we are back in Arkansas. If you want to move again, I will always be by your side."

"I don't know what would be best for us," Zolie finally said. It is surely something to think about."

Zolie and Rosa continued to talk about the discussion they had during the family meeting. One day a few weeks later, Zolie called another family meeting.

"I've thought this over and over and prayed over it every night. We will never get ahead here in the hills so let's put the farm up for sale and leave," Zolie announced. "We could move to some place where we don't have to plow around all these rocks."

"How awful," OlaB said very disappointedly. "How am I going to say good-by to all my friends?"

"You will be alright Sis," Olie said, comforting his sister's disappointment. "You make friends easily. I have also made a lot of friends, but I'm not real close to any of them like you are."

"I don't want to make new friends," OlaB sadly said. "I like the ones I have already made."

A few days later, Zolie announced that he already had a buyer for the farm.

"A family from the panhandle of Oklahoma has bought the farm. They made a down payment of one half the price of the farm and they will pay the other half when they are able to move in," Zolie announced excitedly. "Raymond and Ina Hall are their names. They have two boys and a girl. They didn't say when they planned to move in though."

When the Halls came to take a look at the farm, they came prepared to move in. The farm sold much faster than Zolie had expected and the Edwards had not yet even started looking for another place for them to move into. Zolie wasn't ready to move out of the hills just yet. So he told the Halls that it would take a week or so for them to find a place to move into and he told the Halls that they could move in with them.

The two weeks could not pass fast enough. The Halls didn't buy any of the food and didn't help clean up after themselves. They would sleep late and eat breakfast after the kitchen was cleaned. In general, they expected to be waited on as though OlaB and Rosa were their servants. Richard, the middle son, would corner OlaB and try to fondle her. OlaB tried to avoid Richard as much as she could. OlaB had not told any of her family about what Richard was doing, but she finally told Richard off. But, he acted as though he didn't know what she was talking about. OlaB finally told Zolie and he told her that they would not be there much longer and to try to stay out of his reach.

At one of the weekly parties, Richard came up and put his arms around OlaB in front of all the other kids and wouldn't stop until OlaB had let him 'have it' verbally with both barrels. Richard's sister, Edith, got upset at the confrontation and went home and told Ina, her mother.

'Uncle' John, an elderly gentleman, lived by himself in a large house. He was lonesome and when he heard that the Edwards were needing a place to live, he asked Zolie if they would like to move in with him. The Percifields lived within walking distance and Thelma and her dad would come over every other night or so and play cards. 'Uncle' John loved to play cards and enjoyed the company. The custom developed that Rosa would prepare their dinners and the Edwards, Percifields and 'Uncle' John ate together.

The Halls were supposed to pay the other half of the payment on the farm when they moved in but after two weeks they still had not paid. Zolie waited a little while longer, then told them that they would have to move out if they didn't pay the second half. After several attempts to collect the second half of the payment for the farm, Zolie forced the Halls to leave and the Edwards moved back to the farm.

Edith Hall had noticed the growing attraction between OlaB and Lawrence Sawyer. She had tried to get Lawrence to go with her but he was not interested. Edith was jealous and began spreading rumors about OlaB and Lawrence. OlaB's close friend, Thelma, overheard the rumors and came to tell OlaB. OlaB was embarrassed by the rumors but thanked

Thelma for letting her know. Some of the rumors Edith was spreading about OlaB and Lawrence would not happen between hill couples.

About a month after the Edwards had moved back to their farm, Rosa and OlaB were alone at home when they looked out the front window and saw Ida and Edith Hall determinedly trudging up the road.

"I was surprised to see the two of you coming up the road," Rosa said as she invited them in. "What brings you this way?"

"We just wanted to talk to you and hope that there were no bad feelings between us," Ida replied.

OlaB was not in a visiting mood so she went into the kitchen and started preparing dinner. Edith followed her.

"Why are you so quiet?" Edith asked. "Has the cat got your tongue?"

"I am very upset about the gossip that you have been spreading," OlaB said, still boiling mad about what Edith had been telling everyone. "You have been telling lies about me and I don't like it. I should tell everyone around here what a gossip you are."

Edith jumped up yelling and said. "If you don't shut up I am going to slap your face."

"If you feel like it, you can go ahead and try, but I will wrap a chair around your head," OlaB shouted.

Ida and Rosa came running into the kitchen when they heard the commotion. They both were saying "what's wrong?" OlaB began to explain what had happened but Edith cut in and said that nothing was wrong and that she hadn't said anything.

Ida Hall listened to both girls then said. "Well, Rosa and I will just go to the Danner's and Lucille will tell us that OlaB is a liar."

When Ida and Rosa arrived with the two girls, Bertha, Lawrence's mother was there visiting. Ida was not aware that Lucille was Lawrence's aunt and the Danner's were his grandparents. Soon Ida learned that she and Edith were not among friends and left in a huff. A few days later the Halls moved out of the hills.

*****

Now that the Halls were gone and the farm was back in the Edwards' hands, Zolie began making plans for the next year's crops. He made arrangements with a man who owned a canning factory about eight miles away. He told Zolie that he would buy all of the tomatoes that they could raise. Zolie planted nine acres and Edd Percifield planted five acres. Edd's brother-in-law also planted tomatoes.

Zolie loaded his truck with the first picking and took them to the factory. The factory owner took them but told Zolie that he could not take any more. After discussing the disappointing news with the owner, he learned that the factory was going out of business.

Zolie returned home with the bad news. What were they going do with 20 acres of tomatoes? Zolie, Edd and his brother-in-law went to every grocery store in the area trying to sell the produce. No one had the money to buy fresh tomatoes.

Edd's brother-in-law owned a 'Jot-'Em-Down' store and Post Office in Strickler, Arkansas, about 11 miles south of Prairie Grove. He had a machine that was designed to secure a top to tin cans. He invited Edd and Zolie to get together and can the tomatoes. They set up a canning workshop on the banks of a spring-feed creek and canned the tomatoes. They would pick *one* day and can on the next. Each person peeled and then put the cooked tomatoes into cans to be sealed. Zolie was able to find a buyer for the canned tomatoes at one dollar per case of 24 cans.

The Edwards family was back home on their farm and Zolie was still looking for a buyer. He was now more determined than ever that they should move someplace where he could make a decent living. He questioned whether such a place even existed!

Chapter Twenty Nine

During the early thirties, making a living was getting harder and was not getting any easier. The hill people had started making railroad ties to help supplement their income. It was becoming more difficult for them to sell the railroad ties because the railroad companies were also running out of funds. These ties had been hewn out with axes from timbers on their farms.

Zolie and Olie decided that they would use a two man cross-cut saw to expedite the process. This made the work go faster and somewhat easier. OlaB was watching her dad and Olie and she began begging Olie to let her have a try in helping their dad.

"Olie, let me help Pop, you get to have all the fun," OlaB kept insisting.

"OlaB, you can't do this, you're not strong enough," Olie loudly replied. "Besides this isn't fun, it's all hard work."

"But, I want to try anyway, Olie, and you quit trying to boss me," OlaB stubbornly returned.

Her dad decided to let her try, but after a few pulls, Zolie quit, saying that it was hard enough to pull the saw but to also pull OlaB was just too much!

The mounting economic unrest on the outside was also beginning to creep into the hills. Zolie and his family could see that the country was changing when they left the hills to pick cotton in West Texas and during their picking of strawberries in Louisiana. A big problem was that there were a lot more people on the road ready to hi-jack unsuspected motorists.

In the spring, the Edwards family left the hills for the strawberry harvest. After avoiding several bushwhackers on the road, they made it to the farm where they had worked the previous year. On the last day of picking, a young farmer named Oscar Green, approached Zolie. He asked Zolie if he and his family would pick the strawberries on his farm also. He gave Zolie directions to his farm and Zolie figured that they could make it there before dark; however, the farm was located down a long bumpy logging-road and dark had come by the time the Edwards arrived. The farm house was small and the yard was grown up in tall weeds.

The arrangement had been that a cabin would be provided for them; but, when Zolie and his family arrived, there were no empty cabins available. The cabin that the Edwards were to move into was still occupied by a family that had previously told the farmer that they were quitting but they had not yet moved.

Oscar told Zolie that they could put their bedding on the floor of his house for the night and he suggested that Olie could set up his cot in the cook shack. Zolie looked over the sleeping arrangements and got a tarp out of the truck to place their bedding down on. They surmised that the farmer must have raised chicks in the room while he built their hen house. He had not thoroughly cleaned up after the chicks. What a mess! The smell was awful but Zolie, Rose and OlaB were tired and decided to try to make the best of it for one night.

About two in the morning, OlaB awoke at the meowing of a cat that seemed to be in the room with them. The house had been papered with new building paper and tacked every 18 inches to the celling rafters. The cat was in the attic walking on the rafters with nothing but the paper between her and the room below. Suddenly, the cat missed one of the rafters and came tumbling down on OlaB's head. OlaB tried covering her head with the blanket and when she pulled it over her head, all of their feet and legs were exposed. Finally the cat ran out of the room, leaving Zolie and Rosa laughing at their predicament. OlaB did not think that this incident was funny at all since she was deathly afraid of cats. Needless to say, none of them got any sleep for the rest of the night.

The next morning, they were up early and were out in the cook shack, cooking breakfast and telling Olie about their night's ordeal. After breakfast everyone gathered on the back porch of the farm house, watching a rooster in the yard as he dug for worms. All of a sudden, the roaster fell over dead. Oscar ran to see what had happened to his roaster and saw a rattlesnake slithering off in the weeds. His rooster must have been bitten by the rattle snake. Zolie and Olie could not get the truck packed up fast enough and they were soon on their way back to the Arkansas hills! Another time in the lives of the Edwards....

"It's good to be back home," Zolie said, sitting down after he and Olie finished unloading the truck. "I still don't think that we have a future here though. We are just not getting ahead, I think that we can do better."

"Are you still thinking about selling the farm again?" Rosa asked. "I can be happy wherever we go. I'll admit we do have friends here and know that they will certainly be missed."

"I think that I'll try to find a buyer that has all the money this time," Zolie replied, remembering the problems that they had with the Halls.

In a few weeks, Zolie announced that the farm had been sold, and that they would be moving shortly. About the same time that Zolie sold their farm, the Percifield's house caught fire and burned to the ground. They were able to save only a few of their personal belongings. The community got together and built a house for the Percifield family and refurnished what had been lost in the fire. By the time the Percifield's house was finished and ready to move into, Zolie got word that the buyers of his house were ready to move in, so the Edwards family would have to move.

"Why don't you and your family move in with us," Edd Percifield offered, when he heard that the Edwards' farm had sold and that they would have to move.

"Thanks, but that would just be too much," Zolie said. "You don't have a lot of extra room in your new house. Don't worry about us, we will find something."

"You will do no such thing," Edd replied. "We will make do. You can store your stuff with us. We will set up your and Rosa's bed in one of the rooms, ours in another, and our girls, OlaB and Thelma, can share another room."

"Olie can put a cot anywhere," Zolie said. "We will be happy to share your hospitality for a short while."

Soon, one evening after super Zolie asked, "Edd, why don't you and your family move somewhere where you make a decent living? I hear that there is some good bottom land in Oklahoma."

"I'm afraid to move out of the hills," Edd responded. "I have lived here all my life, and raised my family here. I don't know if I could make it on the outside?"

"Edd, I know that you could," Zolie replied. "You are a hard worker, and I know what it is like on the outside. You would not have any trouble making it in another place."

After continuing to discuss life outside the hills, Edd said that he would think about moving to Oklahoma but that he wanted to sleep on it. Only a few short days later, Edd told Zolie that he and his family had decided to move to Oklahoma and farm cotton.

Edd and his family moved to Stigler, Oklahoma, and looked for a farm to share-crop. This way, they could get started and the owner would furnish the farm stock, seeds, and feed. The farming arrangement was that Edd would give the owner a third of the corn crop and a fourth of the cotton crop. This sort of arrangement worked for many families and farmers during these hard times.

Zolie had asked Edd to look for him a farm also but Edd could find only one farm, so Zolie insisted that he take it and to continue looking for him a farm. Zolie rented a large truck to move Edd and his family to Oklahoma and Zolie and his family would continue living in their house until time to go to west Texas to pick cotton. Zolie told Edd that they would stop by Stigler in the fall on their way to Texas to pick cotton. Their trusted neighbor, 'Uncle' John told Zolie that he would take care of the Edwards' stock and what little furniture that they had while they were away picking cotton.

The next spring when it was time to leave for Louisiana, OlaB became ill. Rosa decided she should stay with OlaB in Arkansas when Zolie and Olie left for the strawberry harvest. OlaB developed a high fever and Rosa got very concerned that she might have some terrible illness. Rosa walked to a close neighbor that had a car and asked them if they would take her and OlaB to the clinic in Prairie Grove. The doctor diagnosed OlaB with an ulcer that must have been infected but said that the only thing to do was for her to stay in bed. Having gotten a letter from Rosa about OlaB's poor health, Zolie and Olie returned home early to check on her. Zolie was not satisfied with what the Prairie Grove doctor had said so he began asking around for someone that might have a better cure. He heard about a young man who had just moved his family back to the hills after having recently graduated from college. He wasn't yet practicing medicine; however, he told Zolie that he had studied about some medicine that would help OlaB and that he had some of it. So he gave OlaB some of the medicine and she soon was feeling much better.

With OlaB feeling better, the four of them headed back to Louisiana to finish the strawberry harvest. When they got there, a large gypsy group had taken over the camp so Zolie found an empty house about a half-mile from the camp. Zolie and OlaB partnered and Olie partnered with Rosa so that each woman would have a man available to carry the heavy boxes of strawberries. When the harvest was finished in Louisiana, Zolie and his family followed the berry harvest though Arkansas and into Missouri. The harvest ended near Saint Louis. OlaB was still was not feeling strong but she had made it to the end of the harvest season.

"I need a rest," Zolie announced the day after the harvest was completed. "Pack up and we'll go to Saint Louis and visit our kin and rest up for a week."

"That will be good for us, we all could use a good rest," Rosa said. "We can visit your mother, and sister."

"We may never be this close to visit them again," Zolie continued. "We can also see my brothers, and after we visit for a while, we can head west to Idaho for the potato harvest."

When the Edwards arrived at the St. Louis camp-ground, they found that the camp was packed to over-flowing, so Zolie went down to the stock yards in hopes of setting up their tent there. The stock yard had a few other campers but not nearly as many as the camp-ground. The stock yards furnished wood, water and an outhouse. Olie soon got a fire started and Rosa began fixing supper.   It was1934, and people were getting more desperate by the day to just survive. Many were out of work with no opportunity of finding a job. Violence was becoming rampant. People would do about anything to just get by. Two men, Joe and Lance, had joined them in the berry harvest in Arkansas and when they learned that Zolie was planning to go to Idaho, they asked him if they could hitch a ride with him and his family when they started west. Zolie was happy to have two extra men when they began on their long westward journey.

After finishing supper, Rosa and OlaB cleaned up and Zolie put the chuck box and cooking pans under the truck along with the two men's bed rolls and they all walked into town. Shortly after they left for town, another traveler came in and parked his car on a small hill just a few feet behind Zolie's truck. Before long, the Edwards returned and went to bed. Then Joe and Lance unrolled their bed rolls and went to sleep under the truck.

Not long after everyone had gone to sleep, two other men from the camp quietly slipped up near the front of the truck with the intent of robbing the Edwards' camp. Their whispering awakened Zolie, and at about the same time, the man in the car spotted what was about to happen and yelled loudly. He looked up and saw Zolie at the back of his truck with his gun trained on the two would-be robbers. With the noise and commotion, the would-be robbers hastily turned around and ran back to their camp. And, luckily for them, they left camp the next morning before day-light.

The trip to Idaho passed without incident. When they arrived in Idaho, they discovered that it had been very hot and dry. The potato harvest was a disaster, to the point that there would not be a harvest at all, much to Zolie's dismay. The very hot weather had caused the potatoes to rot in the ground. It was a little early for the cotton harvest in Texas, so, Zolie packed up his family and started back to Arkansas.

Zolie looked for a farm to rent until Edd could find a place for them in Stigler, Oklahoma. Zolie found a farm to rent nine miles from Mulberry, Arkansas. The family was glad to be in a house again, especially OlaB. The farm was in the community of White Rock. The house was far back in the 'bojacks', but the nearest neighbors were within walking distance. The people in the White Rock community were much like the people that they had left back in the hills near Prairie Grove.

Almost everyone, especially the young people, met in the school house on week-ends. Especially when there was a revival to go to. The community was astonished by what they heard when the preacher began to speak. They had never heard preaching like that before. Some of the people got very upset by what the preacher was saying. Some argued with him while he was speaking. The preacher was always able to give the scriptures to justify what he was teaching. Still some were not happy with what the preacher said. Zolie and his family agreed with what the preacher was saying. It was just what they had been studying during their Bible studies at home. After hearing the preacher for three nights and studying more when they got home, the Edwards family were all baptized in the little Mulberry River, along with eleven others.

There were several itinerant restoration preachers such as, Curtis Porter, who were going around many rural communities in Arkansas, Oklahoma, and other Southern states preaching the Gospel. The Church of Christ, as written about in the book of Romans 16:16, was beginning to flourish during this time.

Zolie made arrangements to move all of their furniture into their new home in White Rock. Their friends, Will and Faye Gasbar, were wanting to move out of the hills and when they heard that Zolie was near, they contacted him. Zolie was there making arrangements with 'Uncle' John to pick up their furniture.

"Zolie, I am glad that I caught you before you left," Will Gasbar said. "We are wanting to move out of the hills and I know that you have a lot of experience on the 'out-side'. Do you think that we could make it on the outside? Do you know of a place? Would you be able to help us find a place to live out of the hills?"

"I am here making arrangements to pick up our furniture," Zolie answered. "I would be happy to help any way that I can."

They sat and visited with Uncle John for an hour or so longer.

"I had better get on the road," Zolie finally said. "Will, you and Faye can load your belongings in the truck with ours. We have a lot of room for the two of you to live with us for a while. You can care for out stock while we are in Texas. Edd Percifield is looking for us a farm in Stigler, Oklahoma, and we will be moving there as soon as we can. I am getting really tired of having to move from Louisiana to Texas and back again."

*****

Zolie got the truck loaded, with Olie's help, for the trip to Texas. They planned to go through Stigler, Oklahoma, on their way and check with Edd Percifield. Zolie hoped that he would have some good news about a farm that he could rent. OlaB was excited to see Thelma again and catch up on what she was doing. OlaB was very happy for Thelma when she told her that she and Robert Cross, a young farmer that lived near them, were seriously dating.

On one of the stops for fuel after their visit with the Percifields, Zolie began talking to some folks that had been on the road for a while and had developed the 'itch'. Olie came over to where Zolie was and began shaking hands and listening to their stories about the road. Later that evening, they realized that they had contracted the dreadful ailment from the family that they had been visiting with. Luckily, they recognized the symptoms and did not contaminate OlaB and Rosa.

The remedy for this condition was made by making a salve from sulfa and lard. This was applied as a poultice to the affected areas of the body. It was a very foul smelling mixture, but it seemed to work after several days. Zolie and Olie would bathe every night in lye soap and water and then would rinse in a solution of Lysol and water. Both treatments burned their skin as they bathed in these 'cures' and their yells could be heard over all the other night noises.

Zolie talked to a druggist after arriving in Texas, and the druggist had just gotten a shipment of salve that would cure the itch. The entire Edwards family was very relieved that this cure had been found, especially Zolie and Olie.

That year was a bad one for everyone. The Purnell's cotton crop, as well as other cotton crops in West Texas, proved to be very sparse, due to the dry and hot weather. It wouldn't take long to harvest their entire crop. Besides Zolie's and Olie's ailments, Rosa began to have trouble breathing and was diagnosed, by a doctor in Wheeler, Texas, with having an untreatable heart condition. Zolie and the whole family was devastated and had a hard time accepting the diagnosis. Zolie began searching for another doctor. He asked everyone that he knew and finally someone told him about a doctor in Shamrock, Texas. So, as soon as Rosa got enough strength, he and Rosa started for Shamrock. The doctor there treated Rosa for several weeks before she got well enough to travel. The family picked the cotton crop for two more weeks while Rosa regained her strength.   The family made very little money that year in the cotton harvest, just enough to meet expenses and buy a few new clothes. The pure cotton harvest ended early because of the weather turning very cold.

Hijackers made it unsafe to be on the road but Zolie had no choice, he had to get the family home. So, he headed eastward toward Arkansas. People heading east from the cotton harvest were especially targeted because they usually had their earnings with them as they headed home. This made Zolie especially nervous so he made special arrangements for the trip back home. He had Olie and their dogs ride in the back of the truck, out of sight. Olie kept a long iron poker with him and if anyone were to try to get on the truck from behind, he would use the poker as a baseball bat and their head as the ball. At least that was the plan. Since the truck was loaded with all their gear it could not go very fast, especially up an incline, and a person could run and jump on the back. Rosa rode in the middle of the truck seat with OlaB riding by the passenger widow, with a loaded gun between her knees.

At midnight, Zolie and his family left the Purnell's farm. Zolie went cross-country until he came to the highway near Shamrock, Texas. Just as Zolie pulled onto the highway, OlaB noticed that a car up ahead was parked strangely. It was parked sideways with the front of the car pointing toward the highway. As they got closer, Zolie could hear the motor running. The car was a newer model and Zolie knew that he could not outrun it. The car had an empty four-wheel trailer hooked onto the back. Most people would have been home sleeping at one in the morning, but maybe the owners were taking a break to sleep, so Zolie cautiously went on his way. OlaB watched the car as they passed by and they hadn't gone but a few miles down the road when OlaB announced that the car was following them. The car would get up close behind the truck, then slow down and back away. At this point Zolie sped up.

At last, the car passed the Edwards' truck and moved down the road until it disappeared. Zolie finally let out the breath that he had been holding for a long time!

"I hope that we were scared for no reason," OlaB said, with a sigh of relief.

OlaB kept her eyes on the road. The moon was bright and one could see beyond the headlights. OlaB noticed something in the road up ahead in their lane.

"Pop, move over there is something in our lane up ahead," OlaB yelled.

Zolie moved over into the other lane and passed the car with the trailer. It had stopped on the road in the right-hand lane with the lights off.

"That was close," Zolie said. "They were waiting on us and planning for us to run into the trailer hooked up in back of them."

The Edwards went on their way hoping that they had seen the last of the car and trailer. In a few miles, OlaB again noticed lights coming up on them from the rear. If Zolie sped up, so did the car. When Zolie slowed down, the car did to. After a while, the car pulled up alongside the Edwards' truck, leaving only about six inches between the two running boards. Zolie had to keep his eyes on the road so he instructed OlaB to watch the car and to tell him if she saw the car door open.

They drove, with their running boards almost touching, for what seemed to be several miles. Nothing seemed to change.

"I am tired of this," Zolie finally said with frustration. "OlaB, hand me the gun. I am going to empty it into the car."

When the driver of the car saw OlaB hand over the gun, they stomped on the gas pedal and shot pasted the truck, leaving it in the dust.

"I surly hope we have some good news when we get to the Percifield farm," Zolie said as they approached Stigler, Oklahoma.

Unfortunately, when they arrived at the Percifield's, Edd had not been able to find a farm for the Edwards. After visiting for a few days, Zolie and his family headed back to Mulberry, Arkansas, and home.

Chapter Thirty

The morning after arriving back in White Rock, Arkansas, Zolie received notice that Mr. Owens, the man from whom the Edwards had rented his farm, had lost his job in Texas and was going to move back to his house in Arkansas. He, therefore, asked if they could please find another place to live.

"I had not been expecting anything like this," Zolie sadly said when he received the news. "We will have to find a place soon. It is too late in the season to find a good place, all of the good places were rented in the early fall."

Before Zolie could start looking for a new place, OlaB's stomach problems returned. Faye Gazbar was not a nurse but she had lots of experiences working with sick people. When Faye saw OlaB, she said that OlaB looked like she had appendicitis. Zolie and Faye took OlaB to Dr. Greer in Mulberry, Arkansas. The doctor examined OlaB, and after running a few tests, he said that she did not have appendicitis but the tests indicated that she may have an ulcer very near the appendix. He prescribed a home remedy and also put OlaB on a strict diet. After some bed rest OlaB began to feel much better.

Zolie, Olie and Will Gaspar went in search of a place to move. They found a spot of land that had two houses. The places were a mess. Tall weeds and grass grew up around the houses with tin cans and glass bottles strewn everywhere in the yards and under the houses. The windows were so dirty that the sun had trouble finding its way through them.

Luckily, the next day was warm. The two families used the 'hill country' method (a lot of hot water and lye) to start cleaning the houses. They scrubbed the floors, walls and windows. By evening, things were almost ready to move in, things looked cleaner but the houses were left with a strong 'stink'.

It was time to spruce up the houses! Rosa, OlaB and Faye took old clothes and cut them into strips. They used tree bark to dye the strips and then they braided the strips into rag rugs.

When a family moved into a new district, all the neighbors would come to visit and in return you were invited to return their visit. One of the families, Mr. and Mrs. West, came to welcome the Edwards. They were younger than Zolie and Rosa and when the Edwards returned the West's visit, Rosa asked OlaB to join them. Earl Johnson, a lifelong friend of the West's, was also visiting them at the same time. He was on a three-month leave from the Army, before he re-enlisted for another four years. Earl was single, and as the Edwards' were preparing to leave, he asked OlaB if she would go to a pie-supper at the school house with him the coming Saturday. OlaB figured that there would be a large crowd at the pie-supper and that this would be a good way to get acquainted, so she said 'yes'.

On Saturday it was cold but it was also time to plant potatoes. Zolie told OlaB that she could stay in the house, where it was warm, while he and Olie planted the potatoes. OlaB knew that if she didn't help with the potato planting that she wouldn't be able to go to the pie-supper that evening. So, she convinced Zolie to let her help with the potato planting. The pie-supper was a success and OlaB and Earl became good friends and dated for the next three months before he returned to the army base.

A Few days before Earl was scheduled to return, he surprised OlaB with a question. "Will you marry me?"

OlaB thought that Earl was joking. She thought that when he got back to the post that he would forget all about her.

So, OlaB said "Yes." And let it go as that.

A day or so after Earl returned to the army post, OlaB forgot all about him. She wasn't interested in marring anyone anyway. Olie was concerned that OlaB was not socializing and wondered if she might be avoiding boys.

"Sis, come go with me tonight," Olie said, insisting that OlaB get out of the house. "I have some new friends I want you to meet."

"Who are these friends?" OlaB questioned. "You have not wanted me to know much about your friends before, so why now?"

"That's not true," Olie replied. "You've always known my friends, especially the girls I've dated. I want you to get to know Rachel, she's about your age and she has a little brother that's sick in bed with a heat stroke. You have been reading those medical books and maybe you can help him."

"OK, I'll go," OlaB said reluctantly. "I'll see if I can help her little brother."

"I was expecting to see a young kid," OlaB said, in astonishment when she was introduced to Bud Johnson, Rachel's brother. "He's a grown man."

As it turned out, he was not sick. This was just a ploy on Olie's part to get her acquainted with Bud. OlaB found Bud to be interesting and charming and they ended up going to the back porch to visit while Olie and Rachel went to visit in the swing on the front porch. Olie never got very serious with any of his girl-friends but before OlaB left that night she had a date with Bud Johnson.

As was her practice, OlaB went to the mail box every day. A few days after meeting Bud Johnson and much to her surprise, there in the box was a letter from Earl. To top it off, it was a love letter. OlaB began recalling the last conversation with Earl. 'Will you marry me', kept flooding back in her memory. It dawned on her that Earl must not have been joking. She had said 'yes' in jest, but the fact was that she had said 'yes'.

"I am certainly glad that I don't get into messes like you do," Olie said, making fun of OlaB.

"You're my big brother," OlaB said. "Help me, what am I going to do?"

"Just let it ride for a few days," Olie answered. "It'll work out."

After two or three months, OlaB got a final letter from Earl. He had learned that OlaB was dating Bud Johnson and surmised that OlaB didn't really love him, even though she had said 'yes' to his proposal. OlaB later learned that Bud and Earl were related. OlaB felt ashamed at the way she had treated Earl, but, she never saw him again. OlaB continued to date Bud and she soon was a happy young woman again.

Olie and Rachael were still dating and Olie had heard of a place called Devil's Den and some of the young men were planning a trip there to take their dates. Olie asked Rachael and she would be delighted to go with him. Devil's Den turned out to be a fun place to take a date and Olie and Rachael had a good time, as well as did the other couples.

On a cold January morning, OlaB went to the mailbox, as was her normal routine, and she had received a letter from her friend, Thelma. Upon opening the letter, OlaB excitedly ran to the house to tell her parents and Olie that in Thelma's letter she said that Edd had found them a place in Oklahoma. To say that the family was overjoyed would be an understatement! Early the next morning, Zolie and Olie left for Oklahoma. Rosa sent them on their way with fresh fried chicken and biscuits for their lunch.

Chapter Thirty One

The place that Edd had found for the Edwards was owned by the newly elected Oklahoma State Representative from Haskell County and five miles from the Percifield farm. The representative was moving his family to Oklahoma City before the opening of the new representative session. He wanted to rent his farm to a share-cropper who would also care for his stock. Zolie and Olie went to Edd's farm and Edd directed them to the Representative's farm. They met Representative D.C. Cantrell and soon made a deal with him, similar to the one Edd had made. Zolie would farm the land and care for the stock and he would get one half of the sale of the crops.

The day the Edwards moved was a cold and wet January morning. Rosa and OlaB were up by four in the morning cooking breakfast after they had spent the previous day cooking a meal to take with them for their moving day. The early breakfast cooking would give time for the stove to cool down enough so that it could be handled when the truck arrived at 9:00 o'clock. What they had prepared for the day of the move consisted of, chicken and dressing, green beans, potato salad, corn bread, biscuits, and a cake. Zolie had rented a large truck along with a driver to help with the move. Their farm in White Rock was located nine miles off of a gravel road on a 'mud' road. The truck and driver arrived late, finally getting there by ten. When the driver arrived he told Zolie that he had been stuck twice getting from the gravel road up to their farm.

Zolie, Olie and the driver quickly got the truck loaded and by the time they got to the highway it was around one o'clock in the afternoon. Zolie asked the driver to stop for a while and have lunch with them. The driver was reluctant to eat, not really knowing the Edwards, but when he saw how much food Rosa and OlaB had prepared and how good it all looked and smelled, he was more than happy to eat with them.

Everyone was excited to finally be getting nearer their new home. The farm was a few miles off the highway and located on a dirt road that was not much better than the road which they had just left back in Arkansas. Luckily, there were a few people near to help each time the truck got stuck. Finally the road became rocky, so traveling was easier; but, up ahead was a hill which undoubtedly would present a problem. The truck struggled to get up the hill but finally made it. A rocky lane up to the house was just over the crest of the hill.

Zolie and Olie returned the next day to move the hay and feed from the farm in White Rock, Arkansas. It was a beautiful day, so while they were away, Rosa and OlaB gave their small house on the Cantrell's property a good 'Arkansas' cleaning since it had not been kept up like a home should have been. They made curtains to fit the windows, placed the furniture in each of the rooms to their liking and were ready to call this new place 'home'.

Soon it was time to make the garden, set the hens and begin their work in the fields. They knew that they would not get to go back to Texas to pick cotton that fall and wondered how they would get by without making any money to buy clothes and shoes.

Rosa and OlaB set and reset the hens by hand and were able to raise 100 pullets to lay eggs the following fall. The only thing that they had to feed the chickens with was the corn from their crop which they had made the previous year. While the chicks were too young to eat the corn kernels, Rosa and OlaB used old overalls, folded them in rows, placed the corn kernels in the rows and hammered the kernels to make mash.

This saved the day by not having to buy chicken feed. This took two sessions each day, one in the morning and one in the evening to have two feedings. They raised two hundred chickens to get one hundred pullets. Soon, they were able to sell all the eggs that they could not use for meals. The roosters sold for fifty-cents for a fryer-sized bird.

The year was now 1936 and one of the driest years Oklahoma had ever experienced. The temperature got so high and it was so dry that year that the rocks became hot enough that they ignited the leaves on the ground. Therefore, the family had to fight fires often. The Edwards kept a five-gallon bucket of water on the back porch with burlap sacks soaking in it. When they smelled or spotted some smoke, they would grab the bucket and run to beat out the fires.

That spring, Zolie planted cotton and corn but the government placed restrictions on farmers. Zolie was only allotted nine acres of cotton because the government decided that limiting the cotton supply would help raise the price. This was a devastating time causing many families to have to wear ragged clothes and worn out shoes.

The Edwards family's 'good' shoes developed holes in the toe and Rosa and OlaB had to sew up the shoes before going into town on Saturdays to sell their eggs and cream. This had to be repeated each Friday evening since the repairs were not long-lasting.

That spring they had a very good garden, but the corn and cotton crops needed summer rain to produce and the rains never came. They kept working the fields and praying for rain. They could hardly stretch the cream and egg money to buy enough feed for the cows and to buy a sack of flour and sugar for their cooking needs. The family could buy syrup and honey very cheaply so Rosa and OlaB learned to cook with those.

The government tried to regulate the price of beef and pork by limiting the supply. A person could sell a calf for $1.00 but if you sold it to the government to be destroyed, the amount you could get was

$10.00. So, people sold their animals to the government to be destroyed and as the farmers stood watching the government burn their animals they became more and more disturbed. To avoid a riot, the government started butchering and canning the meat and giving it to whomever needed it.

One of the Edwards' neighbors owned his farm and got on WPA (Works Progress Administration) program so he had a larger cotton allotment than Zolie had. This farmer had loaned Zolie some money for cattle feed so the farmer hired Rosa, Olie and OlaB to hoe his cotton fields to pay back the loan. The three worked a week from sun-up to sun-down for 50 cents day and they got the bill paid.

Times were not improving. The family was still in dire need of money, the crops had failed to grow, and they knew that they could not go to Texas to pick cotton for their clothes money. They made the decision to contact Zolie's brother, Noah. He managed a farm in Arkansas for a banker who was issued a large cotton allotment. Noah sent money for them to catch a bus to the farm and he told them that he would pay them for helping in the cotton fields.

After a long and tiring bus trip caused by having to make a misdirected and unexpected layover in Memphis, Tennessee, the three Edwards spent a restless night there in a hole-in-the-wall hotel room. The next morning they caught yet another bus to Blytheville, Arkansas. Finally, they were picked up from the bus station by Uncle Noah. They worked tirelessly morning until evening for enough money to repay their uncle for his transportation loan; for their trip back to Stigler, Oklahoma; and to buy clothes and shoes for the coming year.

They wrote to Zolie, telling him when to expect them back home. The bus was delayed getting into Fort Smith, Arkansas, due to an unexpected heavy fall rainstorm, so they were delayed getting into Stigler, Oklahoma, by an entire day. Rosa was delighted to see Zolie standing at the bus stop, waiting for their arrival home. He had met the bus for two consecutive days, being anxious to get his family back home. After this misadventure the family made the decision to never again be separated from each other.

It was very good to be home. Things were finally looking up. It had rained and Zolie had already planted a fall garden, the hens had begun to lay and the cows had calved. Since the cotton had not fully ripened because of the lack of rain, Zolie had decided to pick the small amount of cotton that had developed and he had been able to buy himself some new clothes and a new pair of shoes. Zolie knew that Rosa and Olie could make enough picking cotton for their clothes and he figured that OlaB could do the same. He was not sure that they could make enough for his clothes also, so he had used what little money he got from their cotton and bought a new pair of overalls, a new shirt and some shoes. Rosa had written Zolie a letter saying that she and the kids had gotten some new clothes and a pair of shoes each and that they would shop for him when they got home. Zolie never got the letter.

*****

Olie and OlaB soon discovered that the young country kids in Oklahoma, were like the young kids in Arkansas. Their customary week-end-get-togethers were held in the local district school house almost every Saturday night. But that was as far as the likeness went. The kids in the Sand Ridge District were more like the kids in Texas than those in the Arkansas hills. Olie and OlaB had gotten acquainted with the neighbor's son and daughter. The daughter's name was Celeste Ary and she was OlaB's age and her brother was a year or so younger. Celeste also had an older brother, Bill who was home from the CCC camp (Civil Conservation Corps).

Word got out that there was a party in the neighboring district, five miles away. Bill asked OlaB to go to the party with him. She said that she would if Olie, her brother and Joan, Olie's current girl-friend, could come with them. There was always a lot of games and singing to look forward to at these parties and everyone always had a good time. All during the party, two of the local boys in that district kept pestering Joan and OlaB for a date. They never noticed that OlaB and Joan had actually come there with dates. OlaB and Joan kept putting them off until they had a chance to talk to Olie and Bill. As the party was winding down, OlaB approached Olie.

"Olie, Joan and I are getting tired and don't want to walk all the way home. If you and Bill will go along with our idea and follow our lead, I think that Joan and I can get us a ride," OlaB said, while explaining their plan.

Bill and Olie agreed with the plan. Then the girls told the two boys that they could take them home but they would have to let their two brothers ride along in the back of their truck. The two local boys agreed and were so pleased that they had gotten dates that they never even looked at Olie or Bill. Neither Olie nor Bill looked enough like Joan to be her brother. Bill had blond hair and Olie was blue-eyed and had a light completion. Joan was half Indian and had a dark brown completion and long black hair. Neither Olie nor Bill looked anything like Joan.

They all had almost arrived home before the two local boys were able to put two and two together. For some reason, they kicked OlaB and Joan out so Olie and Bill, seeing what was going on, quickly jumped out of the back of the truck. The four had a big laugh about their 'free' ride as they walked the rest of the way home.

Bill soon went back to the CCC camp and Olie began to soon date a new girl, Evelyn Dobson. Since Bill had to return to the camp and Olie soon started dating Evelyn, Bill and Joan were soon forgotten…

Zolie and Thomas Dobson, Evelyn's dad, both worked for the WPA when they weren't working on their farms. Evelyn had seen OlaB and her family and knew that they were new to the community and wanted to invite OlaB and her brother to a wiener roast the coming week end. Evelyn sent a note by Thomas, her dad, and asked if he would see that OlaB got the invitation.

During the wiener roast, the group of young people formed a club called 'The Midnight Ramblers'. They decided to write skits, small plays and musical routines. Olie and OlaB fit into the group from the start. Olie would play the guitar and Evelyn would sing. In one of the plays Olie and Evelyn would have a wedding. They began dating steadily after that.

Olie and Evelyn had dated long enough that Olie knew he did not want to date any other girl and he wanted to settle down. Evelyn was a very pretty and desirable young woman and Olie knew in a short time that she was the one for him.

Olie told his Dad that he wanted to get married to Evelyn, so he asked Zolie if he would find another place so that they could farm together. Soon Olie and Zolie went looking for a large farm with a larger cotton allotment. They found a farm located in a small valley south of Stigler. It had a large farm house which was located along a graded road on the level valley floor. A smaller older two-room house, which needed some loving attention, was located next to a dry-creek-bed before the road meandered up the other side of the valley. Zolie and Olie both thought that this farm would be just the thing that they needed.

"Pop, I think this arrangement will work out for us just fine for now," Olie said. "Do you think the owner will allow me to fix up the small house a little? I know you and I can make it look more livable and I want Evelyn to be happy here."

Epilogue

Olie Edwards and Evelyn Dobson were married about a year after Olie had asked Evelyn to be his bride. Before their marriage, their custom had been to meet each other in town on every Saturday afternoon. Most locals took advantage of these Saturday outings as a time to visit with each other and catch up on the latest news. On one of those occasions, Olie and Evelyn were making plans to be married on the following weekend, which would have been Easter. But, since they were already both in town, Olie decided that he wanted to get married immediately and he asked Evelyn what she thought of his idea, she agreed that it was a wonderful plan.

Olie and Evelyn, along with OlaB and Zolie and two other witnesses, went to the Court House in Stigler, Oklahoma. After locating a Justice of the Peace, on March 29, 1937, they were married. After the ceremony Olie and Evelyn went to a movie as a way to celebrate and spent some of Olie's $2.50—which was his life's savings.

Olie and Zolie continued farming the acreage that they had located and began fixing up the little two-room house, making it look like home. On December 24, 1938, they had their first son, me, Donald Morgan Edwards. Almost four years later on September 22, 1942, their second son, Jerry Wayne Edwards was born.

After Zolie and Rosa moved from the Cantrell farm, Rosa kept in touch with Minnie, the Cantrell's oldest daughter. Minnie and Rosa were about the same age and had a lot in common. In the early 1940's,

Boyd, the Cantrell's youngest son, was in the Army and stationed in Kansas but would be coming home soon. He and OlaB later became friends and started dating and soon they were married. OlaB and Boyd had two girls, Conchita Gayle Cantrell (Connie) born on April 8, 1942, and Bonita Sue Cantrell (Bonnie) born December 12, 1944. OlaB and Boyd's marriage didn't last very long and after Bonnie was born, OlaB and her two small girls moved back to the Edwards' home and lived with Zolie and Rosa. Later, after Connie and Bonnie were married, OlaB remarried and lived a happy life with Ben McDaniel's, on a small acreage in southeastern Oklahoma.

Acknowledgments

The account of the lives of Zolie and Rosa Edwards would not have been nearly as complete if it were not for a diary found in OlaB's things after her death.

The accounts and events in the lives of Zolie and Rosa Edwards are based on true happenings as recalled by OlaB and Olie Edwards.

I want to thank my cousin, Bonnie for giving me my aunt OlaB's diary and my son, Randal for supplying me with an interview that he did for a school project of my dad, Olie.

As a boy, I recall lessening to my dad tell of his travels as he was growing up.

I also want to thank my wife, Virginia, for proof reading, and helping me with organizing

Other books written by this Author

Destiny: Quest for a New World (Book One)

"I think science fiction helps us think about possibilities" says Mae Jemison. *Destiny: A Quest for a New World* not only jumps into the deep end of the science-fiction genre, it provides a plot filled with complex questions about human nature answered in a remarkably transparent way.

Pacific Book Review –

Edwards holds nothing back when it comes to exploring interpersonal relationships and the importance of family and community for the success of this groundbreaking exploration and colonization of a new world.

Michelle Jacobs US Reviews

Kairos: Quest for a new world (Book Two)

"Kairos" takes readers on the continuing adventure of the Destiny crew in the year 2106. The crew explore and colonize the planet Kairos and establish it as their new homeland. However, they are met with many challenges, including learning to exist in the new world with its strange environment and creatures.

Donald M Edwards
De57ve59@gmail.com

Kairos: Quest for a new world (Book Two)

"Kairos" takes readers to the continuing adventures of the Destiny crew in the year 2106. The crew explore and colonize the planet Kairos and establish it as their new homeland. However, they are met with many challenges, including learning to exist in the new world with its strange environment and creatures.

Donald M Edwards
De57ve59@gmail.com